Josep

by

L. R. Hay

A Salted Lightly publication

www.saltedlightly.com

Cover artwork and Salted Lightly logo
© Brian McGinnis

ISBN-13: 978-1-9160770-2-7

To the Friends of Tammie -
all who enjoyed Jairus's Girl,
whether I know you or not

Thanks for your patience!
C. S. Lewis was right when
he said that children grow
much faster than books

I hope you like this one too   x

And I hope
you do!

Love +
blessings,
L. R. Hay x

The Young Testament is

Joseph's Boy
Nazareth and Bethlehem

Jairus's Girl
Galilee

Coming next

That Woman's Girl
Samaria

Joseph's Boy

The Young Testament

Nazareth and Bethlehem

Contents

A Note From The Author

Boogie On Up 1

House Of Prayer, House Of Fun 10

Ever Decreasing Circles 17

The Price Of A Free Lunch 25

The Curious Incident Of The Priest In The
    Temple 32

The Power Of Three 42

The End (Not) 49

And He Will Be Called – Sorry, What? 57

Seasons Of Joy 63

The Runaway Bride 69

When Jamie Was Right 77

Insert Name Here 84

An Angel's Work Is Never Done 93

The Greatest Story Never Told 99

Eleventy Million And One; Eleventy Million
    And Two… 106

The Surprisingly Good Samaritans 113

Much-Too-Little Town Of Bethlehem 119

O, Sheepish Night 126

Fulfilling Some Laws...134

Worth The Wait...140

Micah Strikes Again 146

Starry, Starry Day 154

Immanuel...161

Rachel's Tears 167

There And Back Again 174

You Had One Job 181

Appendix: Prophecies, Dates And Leaky Tents i

A Note from the Author

Hello! It's me.

While I was writing this book, a few people asked whether I really believe that Jamie, our hero, was there to witness these events.

The answer is no. Some people do believe that, but I reckon the Bible would have mentioned him if he'd been around that early. Personally, I don't think he turned up until page 180 of this book. But a story where the hero doesn't appear till page 180 would be, to give it the technical writers' term, 'a bit rubbish'.

Jamie, the way I've shown him here, would doubtless be huffy to think that he was a mere literary device – but I hope that the real James, son of Joseph, might understand.

Maybe I'll find out one day. Yikes!

On with the story...

Chapter One

BOOGIE ON UP

Jamie believed he was really a prince, but that doesn't mean this is going to be a fairy tale. There will be no multicoloured unicorns, I won't be taking you to high towers to rescue princesses, and at no point will anyone kiss a frog. No, Jamie was a very ordinary boy living over two thousand years ago, whose dreams of royalty came from the fact that he was descended from Israel's greatest king. Jamie knew that an awful lot of other people were related to King David – and all of them just as commonplace as him and his dad, Joseph – but he treasured the secret feeling that he was a prince and one day would be able to boss around anyone who annoyed him. And that would teach them.

The country where Jamie lived was scorching hot most of the time. If the Mediterranean Sea were the sideways diagram of a mouth – with Spain and Morocco as the teeth and lips; Italy a sort of boot-shaped cookie the mouth was eating, and Africa doing an excellent impersonation of the chin and neck – then Jamie's land was right at the back of the throat, where the tonsils huddle. Just above where the food slips down the Red Sea to the stomach.

Jamie's bit of it was a small town called Nazareth in Galilee, but three times a year he enjoyed a trip south to Judea for the great festivals. It made him feel very grown up to be so well travelled. Many of the little children stayed at home with their mothers, but as it had been just Jamie and his dad for almost as long as he could remember, Jamie had come along in Joseph's arms since he was a toddler.

I don't know how many years ago you were six, or how well you remember it? That's how old Jamie was, so I'm sure you'll find it easy to believe that he wasn't behaving like a prince right now. He was dancing his way over the wild hillside with his father, performing a psalm from the Holy Writings. It was from a set specially concocted to pass the time when travelling to Jerusalem. Like 'I Spy' or 'Ten Green Bottles' but with rather more meaning, and therefore less likely to make someone want to stuff a sock in your mouth. They were known as the Songs of Ascent, which basically means Going-Up Songs, and with good reason. Jerusalem was on a series of hills, so if you wanted to go there – no matter where you started – the only way was up.

These songs, like all the Holy Writings, were old even in Jamie's day. They had been sung by travellers more times than anyone could count, but probably never in quite the same way as by Jamie and his father.

"'I rejoiced!'" they chanted loudly, then added their own extra bit in a different, more secret voice:

"(I danced and jigged about. I was very happy)"

Jamie wiggled his hips and hopped, keeping an eye on his dad to make sure the actions were being done properly on his side.

"'With those who said to me, – '

(Are you listening? This is what they said)"

That line called for a hand cupped round the ear and an eager expression.

"'Let us go – '

(Go go go go *go!!!*)"

Jamie and Joseph took a leap forward on each word, jumping up and punching the air on the final '*go!*'

Fellow travellers looked over in surprise at the little boy and his long-suffering father, as the scattered groups and individuals tramped across the wide Jerusalem hills – the final part of the long route south from Galilee. Probably jealous of their cool routine, Jamie thought with satisfaction.

"'To the house of the Lord.'

(Ooooh, great idea! Wish I'd thought of that)"

Jamie and Joseph put their faces close together and whispered this, as if it were the most exciting thing they could imagine.

Arms folded, speaking in deep tones, they stomped forward in time with the rhythm:

"'Our *feet* are *stan*-ding *in* your *gates*, Je-*ru*-sa-*lem*.'"

Then they scurried quickly on tiptoe with tiny, squeaky voices:

"(Well, they aren't yet – but they soon will be!)

'Jerusalem is built like a city – '

(Duh. That's because it is one)"

Jamie was proud of coming up with that line, though they hadn't yet found an action that stuck.

"'That is closely compacted together.'

(Ooooh, yes. It's very squished)"

Jamie and Joseph stuck themselves together, pushing against each other and jostling.

"'That is where the tribes go up, – '

(Yes they do, ooo-be-do-be-do. They're going up!)"

This required left hand on hip, with the right hand pointing in a slow sweep across; a move which people who create the dancing for musicals like *Grease* and *Oklahoma!* have often sought to copy, but I assure you Jamie came up with over two thousand years ago. (That was a joke; the real historical James, son of Joseph, didn't actually invent that move. But you knew that, didn't you? Of course you did, you're very smart)

"'The tribes of the Lord.'

(Mmmm. Just look at all those tribes)"

Now the sweep was reversed... and on it went.

Over the years, Jamie and Joseph had developed their very characterful versions of these psalms as a way to keep Jamie entertained, and it seemed to have worked. He could keep them going on repeat for hours at a time – to the deep joy of anyone within earshot – but if it meant his son was keen to carry on walking, Joseph didn't mind. He couldn't afford a donkey to ride, and Jamie was quite a weight now he was six. Joseph was happy enough to join in with the stomping and spinning and ooo-be-do-bees, just keeping an eye out ready to scoop the little boy up and carry him when the batteries ran down. For all his sparkiness, Jamie had been known to drop off to sleep mid-routine.

He did indeed grind to a halt right now, but not for lack of energy. He'd spotted a little stream tumbling at a distance and perked up, springing and hopping over to it like a kid. Like a baby goat, that is – though like a child too, since he was one. Joseph, not being a kid by any definition, plodded over at a more reasonable speed. He was as grateful for a drink as Jamie, but since he carried the main bulk of their luggage, bundled up in bags and blankets, leaping about was less appealing.

Jamie plunged his whole head into the stream, as if his skin were some kind of sponge and he could drink more the further into the water he went. He finally quenched his thirst and stood up, enjoying the sudden splash of cool water onto his tunic. Joseph slurped the water from his cupped hands so that he could still look about to protect his son from random wild beasts. Jamie tutted with impatience at his father's caution, peering through the heat haze to the final hilltop, still hiding the great city of Jerusalem. He was fed up of sleeping outdoors; they'd been walking for days. He wanted to get there tonight! And he wanted the delicious sweet treats he knew Dinah, their landlady, would be making for him right now. She always spoiled him rotten and, to be truthful, that was the main reason he loved to come. Yes, the Temple was very beautiful – and sure, it was a sacred duty to worship God there – but honeyed pastries stuffed with dates, or figs in syrup, or lemon cakes, or those soft, squidgy cubes made of nothing but sweetness... now that was worth a journey.

Joseph drank his fill and they pressed on. Jamie was no longer interested in singing – not now he was almost at the top of the last slope which would reveal the city, perched on its own hill. With perseverance they drew nearer, and there it was! There were the cliff-like walls with their gates, and so many sandy-coloured houses piled inside all higgledy-piggledy. There on the left was the impressive Antonia Fortress, stuffed full of soldiers, from where the Romans ran the country with their own brand of ruthless efficiency. Over on the right, King Herod's palace tried with plastered-on sparkle to seem more important, but everyone knew he was only there because he'd bribed the Romans for support when he seized the throne. History has decided to call him Herod the Great – in the sense of being powerful, famous and rich, not in any meaning worth having.

Beyond the palace Jamie could just see the old town, the City of David, somewhere he felt with a tingle of satisfaction belonged to him. His ancestor David was a true king if ever there was, not an impostor like Herod.

Right on top of the city, like a very glitzy cherry on a sugar-heaped cupcake, sat the Temple. Unfortunately, it wasn't the original one, built by King Solomon (another of the *long* line of kings in Jamie's ancestry). Jerusalem had a violent history, which was particularly sad as the name comes from the Hebrew word for 'peace' – 'shalom'. As Joseph had once tried to explain to Jamie, real shalom is a calm and wholeness deep inside that comes from God, not what's going on around you. But war had never been far from Jerusalem, and even the precious Temple had been destroyed and rebuilt at times. What Jamie looked at now, a golden structure fifteen storeys high, had been built by Herod. He desperately wanted to be remembered and believed that magnificent buildings were the way to go about it. His Temple only lasted about a hundred years, but he certainly got his heart's desire. He has been remembered more than he could have dreamed! Be careful what you wish for.

This last part of the journey was always the quickest, as Jamie marched on with great determination to Dinah's awesome cooking. His father also felt a flutter of anticipation as he drew close to the city God had chosen as his own; the city where he'd shown Joseph's ancestor such favour. And so, strengthened respectively by a love of God and a love of baked goods, Joseph and Jamie made it to Jerusalem and squeezed with many other eager travellers through the Damascus Gate.

Jerusalem at festival time. How can I describe it? First of all, as the psalmist so accurately observed, Jerusalem is built like a city that is closely compacted together (ooooh yes, it's very squished). Tiny streets shot off at crazy angles; upper storeys of tenements loomed over you as if they were trying to join up and make the street a tunnel, and whole houses were squeezed into unfeasibly small spaces as if they would have to hold their breath permanently just to stay there.

And the other thing was, *everyone* was here – all milling around and chatting at an unnecessary volume. Not everyone from the entire world, I grant you, but all who could trace their descent from Abraham, his son Isaac and his grandson Jacob (also known as Israel), the founding fathers of the Jewish nation. Plus, anyone *not* related to them – usually called Gentiles – who over many centuries had decided that they also wanted to belong to the God of the above-mentioned dudes. And that was quite a lot of people. It was a civil engineer's nightmare; Jerusalem wasn't designed for all these folks!

Thankfully, a great many of them camped on the hills around the city and only came in to go to the Temple. They had that slightly superior air of people who camp at a rock festival, rather than wimping out and staying at a youth hostel or B&B. Jamie, on the other hand, had the slightly superior air of one who knows they will be able to wash, eat cooked meals and not have to queue for a bush every time they need a wee. Showers hadn't been invented back then, so they all had a bit more whiff than we are used to, but even so, it wasn't difficult to spot the campers if they came within nose range.

Jamie squeezed his way along the streets, taking backways and alleys in an effort to avoid the crowds, knowing exactly where he was going. Joseph followed with more difficulty, getting snagged on hooks, posts and people by the bundles on his back. They had a booking every festival with Dinah's family in the south of the city, who kept the tiny room on the roof just for them. With all the evidence of fragrant cooking drifting from homes along the way, Jamie seemed to know which delights were being prepared especially for him, ignoring every other temptation.

He rounded the corner in a trance for his first glimpse of their home-from-home and super-indulgent landlady, but he was greeted by the Wrong Welcome. Dinah's daughter Miriam was sweeping the front of the house clear of litter, donkey droppings and lost tourists. Seeing him, she straightened up with a wary look, tightening her grip on the broom. Jamie knew that Miriam *must* be the same age as himself, but she seemed to have been born grown-up and bossy, in sensible shoes. Being near her always made him feel rather stupid, so the answer was obviously to bluff it out and pretend he was way more grown-up than she could even imagine. Jamie therefore stretched himself up to his tallest extent and adopted a casual air – the seasoned traveller who has seen many famous sights and doesn't give a fruit tart for sweet treats or a landlady's hugs.

"You're here," commented Miriam.

"Yes," said Jamie equally pointlessly, glancing at the

roofs across the street with polite weariness.

"No problems on the road?"

"Nothing to speak of," said Jamie, trying to copy what his father might say.

Miriam examined her fingernails. "We heard there was quite a bottleneck at Jericho."

"We cross the river further south," said Jamie airily. "We find it less crowded."

He shrugged, as if a little bored with international travel. And so they would have stayed – with Jamie racking his brains for something to say that wasn't about maps – had Joseph not trudged round the corner to find the two six-year-olds in their maturity face-off.

"Mim!" laughed Joseph. "Look at you – can you really have grown since we were here last?"

Miriam smiled, confident that she could. Jamie was annoyed no one was making similar comparisons on *his* height, but immediately cheered up with the appearance of Dinah. She had heard Joseph through the window and dashed out to greet them, engulfing Jamie in a bear hug with kisses and gasps and praise for how tall he was, and how handsome, and how very grown-up. This was more like it, particularly as the next thing on Dinah's mind was to lead him in to the banquet spread out for him. Maybe not much of a banquet, as Miriam's family didn't have a lot of money. But for Jamie, who wasn't used to being fussed over by anyone like a mother – even if it was someone else's mother – it was more than enough to make him feel amazing.

After a false start, when Dinah deftly intercepted him and scooted him over to the basin, giving his hands a thorough scrub – and then another hiccup, when Joseph insisted on thanking God for the meal – Jamie heaped his plate with food. It quickly became too full, so Jamie piled several of the goodies straight into his mouth. It seemed more efficient; that was their final destination, after all. He had never really seen the point of plates.

Miriam looked across at him with some disdain as she carefully rinsed her hands. She seemed to think he was some kind of baby, not to be able to wash himself. Jamie wondered whether to be offended, as pastry melted in his mouth leaving tender meat to chomp through. He decided not. It would spoil his enjoyment of the meal – and anyway, Dinah clearly enjoyed looking after him. Making sure Jamie's hands were clean gave her something useful to do.

As Jamie watched Miriam choose her food, calm and unhurried, he saw another reason not to take offence. She wasn't really hungry – not like Jamie; not like his father. For all her grown-up ways, Miriam had never done much. She didn't need to travel; she stayed here in Jerusalem while the world came to her. She seemed so clever, yet Jamie realised for the first time that he knew things she didn't, simply because he'd lived through them. Adventure, and heartache, and wide-open skies. Maybe – just maybe – forgetting to wash your hands because you're ravenous wasn't such a big deal, when you've outwitted jackals, or walked till your blisters burst, or flicked a scorpion off your dad's back, or watched the sun rise from a den you built yourselves. Jamie decided to overlook Miriam's unfair disapproval and gave her a nod. Soon the melting pastry worked its charm on her too; she nodded back in an uneasy truce.

Before long Miriam's dad, Matthan, came in from work and they caught up with each other, as old friends should. Jamie fought to keep his eyes open, but the adults' chat was just... too... soothing...

Chapter Two

HOUSE OF PRAYER, HOUSE OF FUN

Jamie didn't know how he got into his cosy bed on the floor of the little upper room, but that's where he woke when the sun crept in and tapped him on the shoulder early the next morning. He made the most of those first few moments, stretching luxuriously and watching the sun dance on the wall through the gently moving screen. He knew what was coming.

Sure enough, there were frenzied preparations once Joseph awoke. He gave Jamie a thorough bath in the wooden tub, sheltered by makeshift curtains on the corner of the flat roof. And then he did the same for himself, scrubbing and towelling so zealously that they both looked like bright red lobsters – if you could imagine lobsters with dripping, espresso-brown hair. And a beard, in Joseph's case.

Then Joseph went rootling around in their luggage to find the clean clothes he had layered with cassia and other spices to make them smell sweet.

Jamie tolerated it with only the occasional wrinkling of his nose. Once they got to the Temple there would be a ceremonial bath to dip in if they wanted, as a token of making themselves presentable to God, but outward show had never had much appeal to Joseph. He was a go-for-it, all-or-nothing sort of person, so there was no point suggesting they could get away with a quick splash on the face and a dab of powdered lavender.

It did feel good to be so very clean, as they went down the ladder to join the others. All the dust and heat of the journey had melted away, and Jamie's aching muscles were refreshed and strong. It also felt good to have a family around. While Jamie sometimes resented people taking Joseph's attention because he was used to having it all himself, it was a change now and then to be a part of something bigger.

"Bye, Mim," said Matthan, giving his daughter a hug. "Have fun playing with Jamie."

Fun? Didn't he know he'd spawned a monster? Miriam's idea of amusement was mending her clothes or totting up the grocery account to see if the prices had changed. If she even *had* any dolls, Jamie suspected she was teaching them to do the same.

"Bye, Dad," said Miriam, kissing his cheek. "I think we're going to the Temple."

It was a gentle correction, had her father picked up on it – but he was heading over to kiss Dinah and collect his bundle of lunch, so remained in blissful ignorance of his daughter's responsible tendencies. Possibly just as well. What father wants to know his child is ready for middle management at the age of six?

Dinah had heaps to do, preparing for the festival the next day, but she was happy for Miriam to go. She fussed and hugged Jamie, giving him some breakfast to eat on the way (actually the breakfast was for all three, but Jamie just *knew* she'd put the nicest things in for him). Then they set off for the Temple.

Joseph strained forwards as they rounded every corner that brought a fuller glimpse. It certainly was dazzling, towering above all other buildings in the city. It was so vast, King Herod had constructed the biggest man-made platform *ever* for it to sit on. (I say King Herod, but let's credit the architects, builders and the ordinary people whose money he took to pay for it)

The intricate carvings and sheer sweep of gold would take anyone's breath away. Joseph could have taken a professional interest in the craftsmanship, as he was an experienced carpenter in his own quiet way. But neither the incredible skills nor the phenomenal cost could lure Joseph away from his real interest: what the building stood for.

11

This was where God had chosen to live, and told King David there should be a home for the Ark of the Covenant and God's actual presence. The ark itself had eventually been lost in the fighting, but all faithful Jews hoped that God was still with them, as he had promised, and that one day he would literally live here among them once again.

Joseph and Jamie burst into the paved area in front of the vast bank of steps that led up to the gates and stopped, as they always did, to take it in. Miriam followed close behind, seeing the wonder on their faces and looking at the building through their eyes. What wasn't purest gold was shining white marble, and what wasn't marble or gold was precious jewels. The elaborate golden vine that ran all the way down from the top of the central block had clusters of grapes as tall as Joseph! It was all very well for people like Miriam who lived there to get used to it. They could drag their rubbish past to take it to the dump outside the Ash Gate, or chat with a neighbour about how Uncle Abram's tooth was bad and they might have to pull it out, without noticing the magnificent building looming over every aspect of their lives. But for Jamie and his dad, no matter how often they visited, that first full view would always grab the breath from their lungs and every thought from their mind.

They stood there, just staring; just thinking about everything that had happened over the centuries. Then, without needing to discuss it, they brushed away the last evidence of Dinah's baking and moved forward as one, climbing the wide steps.

A stream of people were going up and others coming the opposite way in a steady flow: devout worshippers, as rapt as Joseph; priests and Levites who worked there, easy to spot because of their special robes; tourist-types, out to see a wonder; traders, bringing goods to sell to the crowds. They reached the top and swept through the

Huldah Gates, into the wide and airy Court of the Gentiles.

Life itself was larger than life in this courtyard; everything was taken to the extreme. The noise, the excitement, the activity. Jamie always felt you could probably get anything you wanted here. Absolutely anything. God had been very clear he wanted his Temple to be open for everyone to come and worship – a house of prayer for *all* nations, not just Jewish people, descended from the sons of Jacob. So this outer court was free and easy, and open to everyone. 'Everyone Welcome' had slid over time to 'Anything Goes' which meant there was no longer much prayer going on. Merchants came from all over the Roman Empire and beyond to sell exotic food and drink, silken clothes, and animals never usually seen in Judea to buy as pets, like parrots, peacocks and cute little muntjac deer. One wondrous time, Jamie had even had a monkey climb over him and settle on top of his head! It shouldn't have been there in the Temple – it wasn't on the list of animals considered 'clean' in Jewish law, so Joseph had shooed it off him pretty sharpish – but Jamie couldn't help looking around hopefully every time he came back.

As well as the traders in things, there were traders in money. Although most people used Greek or Roman currency in their daily lives, in the Temple you could only offer the traditional Hebrew coins. This meant that the money traders charged – well, whatever they wanted, really; there was nowhere else worshippers could go! Have you ever seen a stock exchange from one of the world's great financial cities, with dealers haggling, shouting and signalling to each other, as the exchange rate or commodity price goes up and down? Imagine that chaos but outside, in a spectacular, sun-drenched courtyard, and without the modern cellphones and huge screens. Instead, people from all over the empire in dazzling, multicoloured robes; herds of sheep and goats alongside doves and pigeons in wicker cages, all bleating or cooing to be free; jugglers, stilt walkers and snake charmers; conjurers who could make a dove vanish fast and your money vanish faster; souvenir sellers touting cheap goods and expensive price tags; fruit sellers, pie sellers and every-other-type-of-food sellers – all shouting to attract your custom – and just about everything imaginable under the sun. *Sometimes* including monkeys.

Tucked away here and there behind a pillar, trying to get a little peace, someone would be praying. That just *had* to be a Gentile. Nobody would attempt that here, in the wildest marketplace on earth, with people tripping over them, unless they had no other choice. This was supposed to be their special place. Jamie knew he should probably feel bad for those still trying to use the court as somewhere holy, but they did look funny. He watched one man muttering with eyes screwed shut and arms clamped round his ears, his forehead all crinkly as he tried to come close to God.

"It's not right," frowned Miriam, looking at the man.

"It doesn't matter," said Jamie. "*We* are God's chosen people. Our father Abraham was picked out by God specially." He was on a roll now, straining to remember what his teacher, the rabbi back in Nazareth, had said.

"Abraham, Isaac and Jacob. And Jacob's sons – Judah, and Levi,... " This was great. He'd got one over on Miriam, now that he'd started the synagogue school, because girls couldn't go. She wouldn't know this stuff.

"And Joseph," continued Jamie, rattling them off casually. "And... and their brothers."

Can you do any better? There were twelve of them. If you've been in *Joseph and the Amazing Technicolor Dreamcoat*, you can probably sing them. (If you can also name their sister without looking it up, I declare you Emperor of the World) Grown-ups too; come on, come on. Here's a six-asterisk break while you try.

*   *   *   *   *   *

"We're descended from them, so we're more special," concluded Jamie.

"You think?" said Miriam. There was something about her that always made Jamie feel she could read his thoughts. "*Everyone's* made by God. Everyone's made in his actual *image*. If you look down on people 'cos they're not like you, you're looking down on God."

Jamie opened his mouth then closed it again, just to have something to do. Dang it all, how did she do it? He knew that. It was the whole Adam and Eve thing, wasn't it? The first people. Right in the beginning bit of the Holy Writings – the very beginning bit of the bit that was actually *called* 'Beginning Bit' ('Genesis' if you want the fancy word). How could he have forgotten?

"Of course," he managed, looking concerned for the Gentile guy. "It's so wrong."

Truth be told, this outer courtyard was by far Jamie's favourite. The Temple was designed like an onion, or those Russian dolls – layer within layer – each ring taking you closer to the presence of God. Somehow, the nearer Jamie got to the holiest bits, the more boring he found it. The Court of the Gentiles was teeming with life, and it was easy to know you were at a celebration. Joseph and Miriam would have been keen to press in, to get closer, but it was always necessary to queue up to change money and buy an animal. While Joseph did that, Jamie had plenty of time to look around and enjoy the less spiritual delights of the place.

Joseph finally got to the front of a bird seller's line, and *finally* declared himself satisfied with the dove on offer (don't get too attached to this dove; I warn you, it's not going to end well). It had to be perfect to give it to

15

God, which meant there was a lot of flapping and feathers and peering under wings and between toes before that point was reached. Once it was, Jamie tore himself away from watching the contortionists whose gyrations had consoled him very nicely for the complete absence of monkeys – and taken all the little money Joseph had given him to put in the offering box. He rejoined his father and they collected Miriam, who was gazing seriously at the ornate fruit carvings on a pillar (working out the spiritual meaning, no doubt, or critiquing the sculpting technique), and together they passed through a gate in the wall to the next onion ring.

Chapter Three

EVER DECREASING CIRCLES

The Court of Women; what a difference! Calm space peppered with shade and secluded corners. No crowds, just clusters of people seated here and there, talking in hushed tones. You wouldn't dare sit down in the outer court – you'd be scared a whole family of acrobats would somersault into your lap. Or a monkey. Or a whole family of acrobatic monkeys.

People were praying here too, individually or in groups, with a better chance of focusing than in the first court. Mostly Jewish women and girls, who wouldn't be able to get any closer to the Most Holy Place – but also their boys and men, if they wanted to pray together as a family before the guys went further in.

Miriam sucked in a slow breath, her eyes alight. This was where she had wanted to get to, and she had no intention of rushing away. Jamie admitted to himself that he was also happy enough, for now. There was something about the tranquillity of this court that was catching, even to a fidget butt like him. He pretended to put his offering into a treasury box, to keep Joseph happy, then looked around to spot one particular person.

The least, the drabbest, the tiniest, the poorest, the wrinkliest and certainly the *oldest* little old lady you ever did see. And probably the most devoted to God. Jamie couldn't imagine Anna young; she looked as if she'd started at eighty, not one, like normal people. Yet Anna had been young, and beautiful – and married, though only for seven years. Her husband had died when she was still young and beautiful, and everyone had said how easy it would be for her to find a new husband. Her father was called Phanuel and her mother was called LaToyah (she wasn't; I made that up because someone wanted me to name a character in this book after their cat). Phanuel and not-LaToyah were very confident they could get another man for her, lickety spit, but Anna had other ideas. She'd heard in the Holy Writings how God looks after widows and orphans – how he himself would be their husband or their father – and nothing was going to rob her of that. She decided that if God intended to be her husband she had better move into his house, so one day she left the home of Phanuel and not-LaToyah and arrived at the Temple with just the clothes she was wearing and a shawl for warmth. And that's where she still was – *eighty-three YEARS* after her husband died – praying, worshipping, fasting and nodding off, propped up against the marble pillars with the shawl wrapped around her. As much a part of the Temple and just as at home as the little sparrows who nested in the roof.

Jamie and Miriam picked out Anna, sitting under a far colonnade, at exactly the same time and turned eagerly to Joseph, pleading "Can we?"

Joseph smiled. "Looking after someone like Anna is the kind of worship God likes best." He got out a big piece of cheese and a honeyed oatcake wrapped in vine leaves; quite tricky when holding on to a flapping dove. (*Please* don't get attached to this dove. Don't imagine it as cute or pretty, with gentle, trusting eyes. I warn you; it's not going to end well)

They took the food and hurtled over to Anna, stopping abruptly as they realised she was at prayer. Anna opened an eye, aware of the sudden stampede of six-year-old feet in her direction, and gave a half smile. She finished what she had been saying to God and waited a few moments in case he might feel inclined to say something back, then she opened her eyes properly with a lovely smile which really was just as beautiful as when she was a young married woman.

"Hello, Jamie. Hello, Mim."

They pressed forward eagerly with their gifts and

18

gave her a big hug. Joseph waited a moment for the children to finish their cuddle before tucking the dove under his arm and also coming forward, kneeling to squeeze her hand. He could remember bringing her food himself, on trips to Jerusalem when he was a child. He was pretty sure she had looked just as old then.

They gave her the food and she tucked it away somewhere. Jamie knew they brought food because there was no earthly use giving her money. She would pop it straight into the Temple treasury boxes, as if they weren't full enough already from the offerings of gold showered in by rich people. Jamie wasn't sure she even kept the food; he wouldn't be surprised if she gave it to a passing priest, but at least it was a way of trying to stop her fading to nothing. Anna looked as if she wouldn't mind slipping off permanently at any time, but if she was still here, presumably God had plans for her.

Anna was well known at the Temple, almost famous – though that wasn't why Jamie wanted to spend time with her. Well, it was a bit, but mostly it was how she made him feel special in a way Dinah couldn't quite do, however many cakes she baked; in a way even lovely Joseph couldn't quite do, however much he cared for Jamie. It was something about Anna's eyes, crinkly from smiles more than old age: deep pools of love. She looked at Jamie in the way he imagined – hoped – his mother might have done when he was too little to remember. Anna hadn't had children of her own, and it was as if she'd decided to take to herself every child since, to make up for it.

She patted the ground close to her, and Jamie and Miriam made themselves comfortable. Anna smiled, and Jamie felt that warmth he craved, like hot, honeyed milk for the soul. If Miriam's stare made him feel she knew every bad thing he'd ever done, then Anna's felt as if she did too, yet loved him anyway.

"We've been talking about the Holy Writings," said

Miriam, just a tad too smugly. "Jamie had forgotten that the Gentiles are made in God's image too."

Anna homed her gaze in on Miriam – warm as a kitten's fur; sharp and penetrating as its claw. Jamie felt Miriam tense slightly next to him as the sharp-yet-fluffy drill plunged into her heart. He was glad someone could have the effect on her that she always had on him!

"I'm sure he remembers now," said Anna.

"Yes, I do," said Jamie. "I think. But the rabbi at home says we are special."

"Oh, we are," said Anna. "But only because God called our ancestor Abraham to trust him and leave everything to go on a long journey, never to return."

"Why?" asked Jamie and Miriam, their eyes round.

"He wanted to separate him from his ordinary life, because he planned to make a whole nation from him – us – who would also be separate. Holy. Set apart."

"Why?" asked Jamie and Miriam, hardly daring to breath.

"Because he wanted, one day, to bring a great and holy king from this nation, who would defeat the enemy and bring perfect peace."

"David!" said Jamie. David was a great king, and Jamie was descended from him. Jamie was a prince, almost, and –

"David was a mighty king," agreed Anna, interrupting Jamie's recurrent daydream. "But the peace he brought wasn't perfect. It didn't even last his own lifetime. This Anointed One we wait for – the *Son* of David – will be something more. God has a big plan. I'm not sure we understand how big."

Her gaze drifted off into the distance as she tried to puzzle it out.

"Why??!" asked Jamie and Miriam, nearly crawling onto her knee to get the answer.

"Because this king's reign will be forever. *And* it will be for everyone; does that make sense? He's coming to

20

rescue us, but he's coming to rescue all the other nations too. How can he defeat everyone's enemy? We all have different enemies. We are each other's enemies, half the time."

Jamie listened, open-mouthed. This was different from the teaching at school. Rabbi Asher had it down pat about the Anointed One: he was going to be an amazing soldier, who would come wading in with a whacking great sword and drive the Romans and their puppet king Herod out of the land. It was one of the few things at school Jamie was sure he understood, though he hadn't yet got his mouth around the correct pronunciation of 'anointed one' in Hebrew ('mashiach' – or you *can* pronounce it 'messiah' if your Hebrew isn't up to scratch. You might prefer 'kristos' or 'christ' if your Greek is better? Joke. Unless you actually do speak Hebrew and Greek, in which case, awesome!)

The whole Messiah thing couldn't be simpler, according to Rabbi Asher, so Anna's take on the story was unsettling. How could this long-awaited warrior rescue the Jewish people from the Romans – and somehow rescue the Romans, at the same time? How could he bless the invaders while he was kicking them out, with said whacking great sword? Jamie sneaked a look at his dad, sitting behind, to see if he looked offended at this interpretation. Joseph was very hot on the scriptures; he would know. Joseph was listening with shining eyes, caught up in the tale.

"We don't understand it yet, but it will be amazing," he said. "It'll be better than we could imagine. The Holy Writings say *all* nations will be blessed through the one who will come from our people."

Again with the blessing, and nothing with the sword. Jamie was sure there was something about a sword. If there wasn't, there should have been – a proper story needs blood – but Joseph and Anna seemed lost in the wonder of it.

21

The dove fluttered under Joseph's arm, trying to get away, and they remembered why they had come. There needed to be blood now, that was for sure, and they all became quite sober at the thought.

Without a word of explanation Joseph took the dove and held it out; not cruelly, but firmly. Miriam gazed at it, almost afraid, and stretched out her hand onto its head. Jamie looked away; he suddenly felt as if he was prying into a private moment. He knew what Miriam was doing. She would be remembering everything she was sorry she'd done since she last came to the Temple, and putting it all on to the poor dove that blinked up at her so innocently. Then Joseph offered the dove to Anna, who did the same – not with fear, but great sadness. What sins could Anna have to put on the dove? Jamie watched her in surprise. She never did anything; she never went anywhere; she probably never even *thought* anything bad. But it took her quite a while, nonetheless, before she brought her hand away.

Joseph, Jamie and Miriam stood. This would have been the time, of all times, to feel smug. Jamie was about to go with his father from the Court of Women into the Court of Israel, where Miriam would never be allowed to go. But he couldn't triumph as he usually would in his astounding cleverness at having been born a boy. Something about Anna's story and Miriam's small and silent transaction with the dove had made him see things differently, at least for now.

As they walked towards the gate, a boy caught Jamie's eye. It was Cleopas, from his own town of Nazareth – still at the synagogue school with Jamie, though several years older. Clop, as he was known to his many, *many* friends, pushed his lopsided, untidy hair out of his eyes and grinned his lopsided, untidy grin when he spotted Jamie. He was with his parents and all his grown-up brothers, plus those of his brothers' wives who didn't have small children to care for back home, and the only one of his big sisters not yet married. They were just sitting down to eat a fellowship meal together when Eli, the father, glanced over and bobbed back up to his feet.

"No! Joseph, isn't it? Peace be with you! What a fortunate meeting. You remember my wife, I'm sure."

And the kind man went around his whole family, introducing them by name. Cleopas, though hard to pronounce was even harder to forget, but the rest became a blur. Jamie hoped there wouldn't be a test.

Joseph looked awkward. He couldn't very well not draw near, since he was being introduced – but he was always sensitive about seeming to want help, since it was hard bringing up Jamie on his own. Jamie could see he was worried it might look as if they were hanging around hoping to be offered lunch. Jamie didn't mind about that; he *was* hoping to be offered lunch. The roast lamb smelled good!

Joseph quickly introduced his little group and was about to scurry off when, sure enough, the hospitality that culture was famous for came bubbling out.

"Please, when you've made your sacrifice, won't you join us?" begged Eli. "We've just given the portion of our earnings for this past year, so we're celebrating God's goodness to us. The more of us there are, the more thanks we can give!"

"That's very kind," said Joseph, "but we should get Mim back to her mother."

"She won't mind," said Miriam.

Joseph was about to come up with another excuse, when Clop's unmarried big sister, who Jamie was pretty sure was called Mary, looked up at Joseph and smiled. Joseph gaped at her as if she'd punched him in the stomach and remembered several important reasons why actually it would be perfectly fine for them to stay. For quite a long while. He couldn't speak, but managed to mutter something that sounded like "Buh... Aj... Tha... We'll... " and pointed to the Court of Israel.

Mary scooched along the blanket she was sitting on and invited Miriam to join her. Miriam was thrilled, whispering something to Mary as she snuggled up next to her. Mary smiled and whispered back; they were obviously going to get on well.

"We won't be long," said Jamie, hoping he too could sit with this pretty lady when he returned.

"Don't worry, we'll save you some food," laughed Mary, and – *there* it was – the look Jamie craved more than anything! A mother's kindness and teasing fun, but from a woman much younger than Anna. Mary was nearly the same age Jamie's mother would have been if only she'd lived. He beamed at her, completely smitten.

Then he and Joseph went through the gate into the next court – the final onion ring for all but the priests.

Chapter Four

THE PRICE OF A FREE LUNCH

It was quite scary, the Temple building itself, when you got this near to it. Impressive from a distance, oppressive up close. You had to put your head right back to look all the way up, and Jamie felt a sick, uneasy sensation in the pit of his stomach as he did so. Was it just that dizzy rush from looking up – with the sun beating down on him, and the burning gold of the huge vine snaking from top to bottom – that made him feel the building and its weighty ornamentation might fall on him at any moment, crushing him to nothing?

But it was beautiful too, no doubt about that. Was this what God was like – beautiful, but seriously scary; too immense and shiny to take in? Since this was where God had decided to live, Jamie supposed it was the closest they could get to knowing.

Priests and Levites bustled around with their work. This wasn't the kind of job you could just decide you wanted to do when you grew up and ask your teacher about the best courses to apply for. Being a priest or Levite was an inheritance; a birthright; a calling – for the male descendants of Jacob's son Levi and *no one* else. The Levites did the heavy lifting, carrying and cleaning. Then the priests themselves – well, that was even more select. They were descended from Aaron, the first priest, who was appointed by his brother Moses – and, apart from the odd blip, the *high* priest was the oldest son of the oldest son of the oldest son... make that dot dot dot stand for as many generations you like, because I'm not sure anyone really knows.

That was how it was supposed to be, at any rate – but where there are rulers like Herod and the Romans knocking about in the equation, things get muddy. They sold the God-given role of high priest, or handed it out to men loyal to them. The current one was a father-in-law of King Herod, not that being related to him made the position safe. At the start of his reign, Herod had made his teenage brother-in-law the high priest, then killed him soon after because he thought people liked him more. They probably did.

But at least many of the ordinary priests were still sons of Aaron – and there was no choice but to accept all this, unless you decided to avoid the Temple and not celebrate the feasts. To someone like Joseph, that was no choice at all.

There were quite a few worshippers wanting to make a sacrifice, but the area in front of the Temple building was spacious enough for it not to feel crowded. There were plenty of priests, too, so in no time at all one spotted them and came over. Now it was Jamie's turn to lay all his sin on the dove, and he tried to get it over with quickly. Usually he felt insulted at having to do this yet *again*, and couldn't see why his dad didn't just put money for a sacrifice in the treasury and let the priests deal with it. Jamie thought himself a fairly good sort of person; he did his best, anyway – and in Jamie's secret opinion, his best was pretty outstanding.

Joseph's patient explanations always went for nothing: that it wasn't so much about what you *do* as what you *are*; something deep in everyone – in human nature itself. The nicest person is still not perfect, and however close to perfection they might seem, 99.99999999999999999999999999999999% recurring is not 100% just the same as 0.00000001% is not 100%.

Somehow, this time, Jamie instinctively knew that, as every little way he'd fallen short came tumbling through his mind when he stretched out his hand. He tried not to look into its eyes; it didn't seem right that this innocent creature should have to go through this for him.

"This is God's merciful provision to you," whispered Joseph, seeing his struggle.

"It's not fair!" spluttered Jamie, trying not to cry.

"No, it's not," agreed Joseph. "But it's love. If God hadn't allowed for this substitute, it would be you and me, Jamie. We have to trust God for the dove; he cares about everything he made, even the plainest sparrows. Give it to God, and be thankful he made this way for you to come to him."

Joseph laid his own hand on the dove's head, and – well, you know what's coming. At least it was quick, with one deft twist from the priest. Jamie watched him carry the pure, limp, scrap of a body to the huge, cube-like bronze altar in front of the Temple building where he touched its blood onto the corners and then climbed the ramp to the top, placing it with all the other sacrifices on the metal mesh above the fire that never went out. Once it was burned up, its ashes would be taken to a place outside the city, where all the sin it carried would finally be forgiven.

Jamie gave a sigh of relief, as if the weight of the holy building looming over him had now been lifted, and Joseph put a hand on his shoulder and guided him back to the Court of Women. That had shaken him more than he expected, but Jamie was confident he would soon be thinking about monkeys and stilt walkers again. And they had been invited to a meal with their new friends! There would be lots to tell Dinah when they got back; he didn't need to mention he had been a bit silly over a dove.

"I hope I get to sit near Mary," he confided to Joseph as they slipped back into the women's courtyard.

"Yes," said Joseph, going glazy-eyed at the thought.

Jamie raced over to the group and sure enough, Cleopas budged up on the blanket to make room between himself and Mary. Joseph sank down opposite, grateful not to draw attention to himself, though Eli welcomed him back and made sure his cup was filled. (Fun Fact: the Greek version of Eli's name was Heli, which at a glance looks short for Helicopter. That could be distracting, so we'll stick with the Hebrew – but I thought you'd like to know)

Jamie launched right in. It was a wonderful meal – to be part of such a big family, all laughing and chatting and passing each other food. Clop was hilarious. Jamie felt great to be joking alongside him; he had never dared speak to him before. Miriam seemed to be enjoying the extra company, too. She didn't look quite so studious as usual, and even giggled a few times. Jamie hadn't been convinced she knew how to giggle. Joseph didn't laugh much – or say much – or eat much – but his shy smile showed he was happy they had stayed.

Everyone gave a tenth of what they'd earned (tenth is 'tithe' in old English) to support the Temple workers. When they brought it, as Eli's family had just done, it included a celebratory meal to share with them, so a Levite family had been invited to join the party. Then an actual priest and his wife came over, and – to Jamie's delight – the grey-haired couple sat in the place of honour next to Eli! Mary explained that her mother was a cousin of the priest's wife, Elizabeth. Jamie had never spent longer with a priest than the time it took to make a sacrifice. He almost expected them to hover above the picnic with a holy glow, not to eat or sit down like normal people. But Zechariah was reassuringly normal and nice. He put everyone at ease, and was particularly good at making sure Jamie, Miriam and Clop didn't feel left out of what he said, which Jamie noted with approval; Rabbi Asher in Nazareth never bothered to talk to children, except when he had to teach. Jamie couldn't help looking around with concern, even so.

"Are they going to bring their family too?"

The Levites who'd joined them seemed surprisingly numerous. This sharing was fun, especially as it was someone else's food, but if Zechariah and Elizabeth brought a gang of a similar size, there might be a danger of it running out.

"It's just the two of them," said Mary. "They were never able to have children."

"Oh," said Jamie, trying not to sound pleased.

He sneaked a look over to Anna as they carried on eating. He would have loved it if they could invite her, but she never joined in these meals. Mary saw where he was looking.

"Anna might be fasting," she said. "Most of her time is spent praying, so she doesn't eat very often."

Jamie knew about people going without food to concentrate on God (though he suspected they'd got it the wrong way round; God would still be there when you finished eating). But he was worried the way Anna never seemed to eat at *all*. He saw that Mary looked worried too. She picked out a tender strip of meat and a piece of floury bread drizzled in olive oil, handing them to Jamie with a cup of new wine mixed with water.

"Why don't you take this to her?"

"She won't eat it," objected Jamie. "She never does. She puts it away, as if she's going to eat it later."

"I bet you can find a way to get her to," said Mary.

Jamie was surprised. Mary thought he could do something even grown-ups couldn't? He was always thinking how clever he was, but it was new to see that someone else believed in him. He went over feeling unusually capable, wanting to live up to Mary's trust.

When he knelt by Anna and held out the food, she smiled in the way he knew was a total fob-off; she was going to tuck it away with what they had given her earlier, and it would *not* get eaten. She stretched out her hand, but Jamie kept hold of it. What should he say?

Something popped into his mind, so he went with it.

"This was given to God by Eli's family," he said. "It's part of their... thingy."

"Tithe," nodded Anna, starting to suspect what he was up to.

"The law of Moses says we have to eat it together, like friends. We have to *feast*. So you probably need to eat it now, while the rest of us are. Just to be safe."

Anna looked at him, amused. She knew exactly what he was doing, but she could also see that there was no answer to it. She laughed. Jamie laughed too, but he wouldn't let her take it till he was sure she wasn't going to wriggle out of it.

"Well, I must eat it straight away then, mustn't I?" said Anna, starting to nibble on a corner. Jamie looked over to Mary and was thrilled to see she was watching. She nodded a 'well done' and Jamie glowed with pleasure. Anna wasn't used to eating such solid food, but Mary had chosen well, and with a little chewing she made her way through it.

"My, that's tasty," Anna said. "God be praised for his provision, and bringing Eli's family safe through another year. Mmm, so good. Thank you, Lord, for fellowship, wholesome food and enough teeth left to eat it with. Mmm, very juicy."

Jamie watched her alternate between prayers of thanksgiving and comments on the scrumptiousness until it was all gone.

"Hoooo! Delicious," she breathed. "I think I need a little nap now."

A little nap was what they all felt like, once the meal was done, so they went their separate ways, wishing each other joy in the coming festival.

Back at their lodgings, Dinah and Matthan were very interested to hear all about the day, and especially the family they had met.

"We weren't going to stay," explained Miriam, "but then Uncle Joseph changed his mind."

"Yes, it was when it occurred to me that we might be under your feet if we came home early," said Joseph.

"It was when Mary smiled at you," Jamie reminded him helpfully.

Dinah and Matthan's eyes slid straight over to Joseph as if they were worked by a string, and their eyebrows shot up enquiringly almost into their hairlines.

"No, no. I don't think so," said Joseph, concentrating hard on the sandal he was polishing. "I just thought we might be in the way here."

"We didn't really know Mary's family," said Jamie. "We hardly saw them in the street, and I never talked to Clop at school. But now we're friends. Wouldn't it be great if we saw them again? I hope we do."

"Yes, Jamie; I'm sure you will," said Dinah, throwing Joseph a Very Significant Look.

Chapter Five

THE CURIOUS INCIDENT OF THE
PRIEST IN THE TEMPLE

Who would have expected that they'd run into Eli
and his family as many times as they did over the week
of the festival? Jerusalem was chokka, and once the
celebration started, the Temple itself was jam-packed
too – even the quietest nooks and crannies. Jamie
thought how lucky they were to keep seeing them. Of
course, it wasn't totally luck; Jamie was looking out for
them very hard. As was Joseph, though he tried not to
show it. Dinah and Matthan seemed to be watching for
them, too. And – don't think me overly suspicious – but
surely, statistically, it couldn't have happened *quite* as
many times, if some on the other side were not also
trying to engineer it? Days when they didn't bump into
each other were unusual, and chance meetings where
they decided they really might as well hang out together
were the norm – with Joseph rather quiet, and Mary on
at least one occasion surreptitiously kicking her middle
brother and going to the other side of the group so he
couldn't tease her, as all the older brothers laughed.

Eli's family seemed to get bigger and bigger, with
Mary's married sisters sometimes spending time with
them rather than their in-laws. Jamie decided it was the
very best way to do a festival, and felt part of things as
he never had before – with lots of grown-ups making a
fuss of him, cool and popular Clop now his friend, and
Mary's oldest brother teaching him how to fold his
eyelids back on themselves to look like a monster.

This was very much as it should be (except the
eyelids), because it was written down as a fact from
God that they *had* to enjoy themselves at these festivals.
How awesome is that, to be told you'd be breaking the
law if you didn't have a good time? This particular feast

was called 'Weeks' ('Shavuot' in Hebrew) because you had to count off seven weeks from the start of the grain harvest – or 'Pentecost' which means fifty, if you preferred counting days – or just 'Harvest' if you couldn't be bothered counting anything.

The idea of a Harvest Festival makes *me* think of cold mornings, log fires, leaves turning orange and brown, and everybody bringing tins of beans or pineapple chunks and singing songs about ploughing the fields and scattering. You might think "Oh, *yes!*" – or your idea might be completely different. Exactly when you harvest the different types of produce depends on where in the world you live, and this Festival of Weeks was in the spring – May, the Hebrew month of Sivan.

After seven weeks of harvesting the barley and wheat (seven sevens, if you think about it – or a week of weeks. Neat, huh?) all was safely gathered in, to quote another of those songs, and everybody brought a token of their harvest to show to God as a thank you. They all waved their loaves of bread at the same time towards the Temple, which Jamie thought was great – as if they were waving to God! He wondered if God was ever tempted to wave back, and how they would know if he did.

Everybody had an interest in the harvest – even carpenters, weavers, ironmongers and perfume makers. Many people owned a little land where they grew crops in addition to their usual work, but even those who didn't still needed the farmers to have a good harvest so they could buy flour from them the whole of the next year. The farmers could be sure of many helping hands to get the grain in before it withered, so most people now felt the achy muscles and deep satisfaction that comes from knowing you've earned a holiday.

The only nasty note for Jamie's group couldn't be helped. King Herod was there. Of course, he would have to reside in Jerusalem *occasionally*. It was too much to hope he would stay in one of his other palaces the *whole* time. He decided the feast was a good opportunity to remind the people that, while they may be here to worship their God, Herod's was the only power that mattered. He had himself carried through the streets whenever he felt like it, lying on a couch, propped up with squashy pillows which perfectly matched his puffed-up face – the jewels glinting like the malice in his eyes. His ugliness did not come from his appearance, which, after all, a person cannot help. He was simply ugly – that was all that could be said.

His guards marched in front and behind. There was more than one way of looking at Roman soldiers: they weren't all bad. Some were ordinary men who had been called up into the army with no choice. Even those who had decided on a career as a soldier could be fair or corrupt, cruel or kind, reasonable or demanding. They could choose to be decent people, as far as their orders allowed. But Herod's guards had already made their choice knowingly, to serve a cruel bully – so how could they be anything else themselves?

Jamie and his group had already managed to avoid them a couple of times, but one day they were halfway down a street with crowds hemming them in just as Herod's party turned into it, leaving them nowhere to go. They pressed themselves to the walls to let him pass, Joseph putting his arm protectively in front of Jamie. Everyone lowered their eyes to the ground – to make it look as if they were showing respect, but really to avoid having to see that hateful face. The last thing anyone wanted was to catch the eye of Herod or one of his thugs. It seemed to Jamie that Mary did catch his eye, even so. Jamie was sneaking a look at him in revolted fascination as he sneered down at the crowd, darting his suspicious eyes around, distrustful even of his guards. The brute stopped his constant scanning to stare at Mary – a flicker of interest on his sweaty face. Jamie felt hot anger rise, staining his cheeks with crimson and his eyelashes with indignant tears. Although he was only six, he instinctively knew this man had no right to stare at someone in that way.

Mary kept her eyes to the ground trying not to move, then Herod grabbed his stomach as if in sudden pain, yelling at his servants to get him home. Good, thought Jamie – as did they all. In the many years since he seized the throne, Herod had not treated his people in a way that would encourage them to pray for his health or a comfortable digestive system. But no one said it out loud, of course; Herod's spies were everywhere.

Thankfully, Herod was soon forgotten in all the happy times. On the last day of the festival, as Jamie set out for the Temple sporting his usual scrubbed lobster look, he felt disappointed it would soon be over.

He needn't have worried. There was a shot of excitement in store for them that booted all sense of anticlimax right out of the park. Eli was waiting near the top of the steps and pretty much grabbed and dragged them through to the Court of Women faster than you could say "What, no monkeys?" There was his family, hyped up with anticipation – Mary's mother and Elizabeth weeping together with joy.

"Zechariah has been chosen to burn incense in the Holy Place!" cried Mary, clutching Jamie and Miriam's hands in delight. "Imagine. Every single one of the priests on duty, because of the feast – and the lot fell to him! Isn't it wonderful?"

"Such an honour!" gasped Eli, out of breath from all the people he'd told. "A priest can live his whole life and never be chosen."

"Amazing," said Dinah, hugging Elizabeth. "You must be so proud! Has he ever done it before?"

"No, never!" said Elizabeth. "Not even on an

35

ordinary day, when only his group is on duty and not many worshippers around."

Elizabeth was also descended from the first high priest, Aaron – although, not having taken the trouble like Jamie to be born a boy, she would never be able to go near God's presence.

"He will speak in front of huge crowds today," said Joseph, awestruck. "Just think how many will hear him pronounce Aaron's blessing on us, when he comes out!"

"Where is he?" asked Jamie, looking around eagerly.

"He isn't here, sweetheart," said Elizabeth. "He's in one of the side rooms, praying and fasting to prepare himself. He has to go into the Holy Place on behalf of all God's people. It's a huge responsibility."

"Then he comes out on behalf of *God*," murmured Mary. "Huge doesn't even begin to describe it!"

Because they couldn't get anywhere near God, he had made it so that the priest could be a kind of inbetweeny person – representing humanity to God, and God to humanity. It wasn't perfect, because the priest wasn't perfect; only God could truly represent himself, of course, but this was God's way of dealing with all those grey areas mankind was so good at coming up with.

Everything in that day's celebration seemed to be building up to the time Zechariah would go in and burn the unique blend of sweet-smelling spices on the beautiful gold incense altar inside the Holy Place itself. As the ceremony drew closer, the excited group of friends approached the Court of Israel. Jamie hesitated at the gate, feeling bad at leaving Mary, Miriam, Dinah and Elizabeth behind with Mary's mother and assorted sisters and sisters-in-law, but Miriam egged him on.

"Go on! You must watch. Get as close as you can!"

Jamie nodded back at them as he went through. The entrance to the Temple was fairly high; they'd be able to see most of this historic moment.

Jamie pressed forward with Clop and the men, until he found himself in the front row. What an experience this was going to be! To know the person going in on their behalf. To hear all about it from him afterwards! No other boys in Nazareth could say that. Jamie doubted if even the rabbi could, or he'd have gone on and on about it. Now, Jamie and Clop would be able to go on and on, and they'd all have to listen. This was *almost* as good as being descended from King David.

He could see Zechariah: nervous at the honour, but holding his head up very nobly. Jamie wanted him to give them a little nod or a wave, but he knew this wasn't the time. People often talk of incredible experiences as something to tell your grandchildren one day. That had always puzzled Jamie; if it was that good, wouldn't you want to tell your children too? But it struck him now that this was exactly that kind of thing; he should try to remember every moment.

Other priests prayed with Zechariah, then he walked up the steps with dignity and into the Temple alone. The huge doors swung shut, hiding him from view.

This was like that bit at a church wedding, when they disappear into a side room to sign the register and you wonder if you're allowed to talk, or get out a bag of popping candy. Everybody stood still, trying to look very spiritual. Fortunately, it wouldn't last long and he'd be out again – spreading his arms wide in blessing, declaiming the words his ancestor Aaron had first said over a thousand years before...

The moment was nearly here. They all held out their hands in prayer to receive the blessing...

This was great.

Although Jamie was glad Zechariah would come back out soon. Very soon...

One or two priests in front of the Temple looked as if their minds were starting to wander...

What a fantastic experience. Jamie wouldn't have missed it for anything.

Even if this part was perhaps a bit boring...

A fly settled on Eli's beard; he tried to ignore it for a few moments, but then swatted it away. Everyone nearby watched in fascination to see where it would land next, while still trying to stand motionless as if they were praying: Matthan's shoulder; Jamie's nose; Mary's middle brother's ear – big mistake on the part of the fly, as he squashed it into oblivion, all splatted into his hair.

Phew, good job that was dealt with; Zechariah would be out *any second* now, and they didn't want a floor show like that distracting them from the big finale. Though the fly scenario had passed several minutes with a welcome burst of entertainment...

The way Zechariah had been chosen was just amazing; what an honour to know him... Yes... How wonderful...

Jamie's arms were burning at the effort of being held out so long. Would it look stupid if he dropped them? He noticed that men and boys here and there were starting to cheat their arms slowly down. Even some of the priests. *Especially* the priests. A consensus seemed to be spreading throughout the crowd to lower their arms, as if that was exactly the amount of time they had *intended* to hold their hands out, and now was the correct moment to bring them down.

This kind of delay just did not happen. What the Hezekiah was going on? Jamie shot a look at his dad.

Earnest man of God though he was, Joseph wasn't bothering to hide his concern. No one was thinking about praying or incense or priestly ritual any more.

"Has he lost the plot?" hissed Clop. "Is he even all right? What if he's ill? – or dropped dead right there in the Temple! Shouldn't a priest go in and get him?"

The priestly posse at the front were shifting uneasily, starting to mutter that very question. No one wanted to break away with a decisive opinion, because then *they* would be the one who had to do it. Go into the Holy Place, when you'd not been chosen? That would be unheard of. Who knew what might happen! But, then – who knew what *had* happened?

Jamie tried to look back to the women's court, but the crowd was too tightly packed. Was Elizabeth coping with the suspense? Surely she must be worried for her husband?

The vast doors with their ornate carvings erupted open and everyone gasped. Zechariah stood there, clinging to the door post, staring at the crowd with an expression of disbelief as if he'd never seen them before – or the walls – or the sky. If he had been an alien who'd only popped down the road for the alien equivalent of a bag of chips, opening the door of his spacecraft to find himself on our planet and a sea of earthlings assembled to greet him, he could not have looked more bewildered.

Well, this was quite something. Never mind the rabbi's school in Nazareth, or any number of bouncing grandchildren – Jamie had a feeling this might be the kind of thing you'd want to tell the whole world. They all gave up breathing, temporarily, as Zechariah edged his way forward.

He spread out his arms towards the crowd. This was promising; he might be getting back on track – though his desperate, imploring expression didn't look as if he'd be pronouncing the blessing anytime soon.

"Why doesn't he say it?" whispered Jamie. "He must remember it. We did it in school:

'The Lord bless you and keep you;

The Lord make his face shine upon you... '"

"Shhh," said Joseph, staring intently at Zechariah. "I don't think that's the problem."

Zechariah opened his mouth but nothing would come out. He pointed over his shoulder into the Holy Place with a look of awe and terror then started to gesture, trying to describe something with his hands – something towering and extraordinary. This was no sickness, or an old man's frailty. Several priests ran to help him.

"He's seen a vision," breathed Joseph. Matthan and Eli exchanged looks of amazement. A vision? – in the Holy Place? – what could it be, but...

Zechariah's attempts to speak became more urgent, and the gesticulating speeded up: something huge, something magnificent! One of the priests peered cautiously through the open door into the sanctuary. He shook his head to the others; nothing there now. They helped Zechariah down from the entrance and over to somewhere private where they could care for him, leaving one of their number staring at the crowd. He raised his hands in the sign of blessing and mumbled his way through the wording, then shut the doors carefully and slinked down to join the others.

That was it. Nothing more to see.

No one in the crowd knew what to do, and there was no direction from the priests. If the high priest had been there, he could have inquired of the Lord to find the meaning of it, but he didn't always bother turning up.

Eli was torn between his responsibilities – to look after Zechariah, or his wife's relative Elizabeth; this must have been an awful shock for her. Joseph saw Eli's difficulty, and that Clop and his beefy brothers

40

were too gob-smacked to be of any use.

"You go to Elizabeth, make sure she's all right," Joseph said, taking charge. "We'll find out from the priests how Zechariah is."

"Yes. Thank you," said Eli. "Poor Elizabeth. Poor Zechariah!"

"We don't know that yet," said Joseph, a strange expression on his face.

He took Jamie's hand, striding along with him and Matthan – not worried, in the way you might expect. Almost excited, Jamie thought as he looked up at him.

Joseph had no idea why he felt so excited. Neither did Jamie. They wouldn't understand it for quite some time; just over nine months, in fact. *Big* clue. Though possibly not the same nine months you're guessing at? Aha. There's going to be more than one baby kicking about, before we're done.

No, they didn't know it, but they had just witnessed the very first event of the Christmas story.

Chapter Six

THE POWER OF THREE

Jamie had never been in one of the little side rooms of the Temple courts before. They were mostly used for storage, or sometimes Anna slept there when the nights were cold. It wasn't as if they were forbidden, but only priests and Levites usually had reason to go inside. Jamie was most definitely inside now, however, with the concerned priests gathered around Zechariah. What a day this was – and it wasn't over yet! Jamie didn't know which part he would tell the boys at school first.

Zechariah still couldn't talk, and his shining eyes were fixed somewhere off into the far, far distance; he seemed unaware of them. When they spoke to him it was hard to tell whether he couldn't hear or was just uninterested in their questions. When they brought him something to write with, he ignored it.

When eventually they felt sure Zechariah wasn't ill as such, Joseph and Matthan supported him on either side while Jamie cleared the way to bring him to Elizabeth. Miriam was keeping a look out, and quickly beckoned them to a corner of the women's court where Elizabeth sat, surrounded protectively by Eli's family. They helped Zechariah to sit on the ground by her, and Elizabeth clasped his hand anxiously. He managed to bring both his vision and attention on to her and gazed in wonder. Tears came to his eyes, but Jamie couldn't tell if they were sorrow or joy. Zechariah squeezed Elizabeth's hand and kissed it, trying to speak with a heart so full it seemed he could never find enough words again. His face broke into a smile, which Elizabeth couldn't help but mirror in spite of her fears. And then he laughed! Pure joy, unmistakable, despite the lack of sound. Everyone looked at each other, not knowing what to make of it. Finally, he stood to his feet without help and walked steadily back to the Temple building. Jamie and Miriam crept part of the way after him and saw him kneel in front of it, worshipping – just him and his God, as if no one else was there.

When they returned, they found there was silence from the friends around Elizabeth.

"What should we do?" said Eli eventually.

"I'm not sure we need to do anything," said Joseph. "Zechariah's group is on duty next, isn't it?"

"That's right," said Elizabeth. "The other priests will go home after the festival ends tonight, but the clan of Abijah will stay to do their normal week."

"What, we just leave him here?" asked Clop.

"It looks like it's where he wants to be," said Miriam, nodding through the gateway to where the old priest still knelt, oblivious of everything but the Temple.

"But he's been taken ill!" fretted Eli. "We can't just abandon him."

"This is not a sickness, " said Joseph. "I don't know what it is, but something of God happened here, and Zechariah seems blessed. I think we can leave him without worrying, and let him serve his duty as – "

He was about to say "as normal", but this was so very much not normal, he trailed off.

"As he would have done," finished Mary. "As is right and fitting for him to do."

"Exactly," said Joseph, and their calm certainty reassured the others.

"I will stay too," said Elizabeth firmly, going to the gate and looking through at her husband.

They left her there and passed Anna on their way out, pacing up and down muttering, doing serious business with God. Anna had the gift of prophecy, which meant that sometimes God would show her what was on his heart. I suppose that's what you get when you spend a lot of time in someone's company. No one but Zechariah knew what had happened, but Anna was on the case to find out.

It was an odd final evening before their journey home, but it drew the group together even more. Matthan and Dinah invited Eli for supper at their house, along with those of his family who hadn't dispersed to their campsite, and they went over and over what it could all mean. Most were convinced that God had done something, or was about to do something – but what? There had been no more Holy Writings added to the scrolls in the synagogues for four hundred years, and no miracles for at least a hundred and fifty. Nobody was used to God doing things now, in their time.

All they did decide was that Elizabeth could stay at Miriam's house while her husband completed his duty, and once it was done, Matthan would borrow a cart to take them back home. They lived in Hebron, one of the towns God had given the priests when the nation first came to this land. It was in the Judean Hills south of Jerusalem, and less than a day's walk for someone strong and healthy – but Zechariah and Elizabeth were getting on in years, and Eli was convinced it had been a seizure and there might be another, so this plan gave everyone peace of mind.

As the evening wore on, with their parents not noticing the time, Jamie and Miriam got into another of their face-offs, seeing who could be the most grown-up by not closing their eyes, not looking bored and not falling asleep in their soup. Miriam even raised the stakes by joining in the conversation occasionally, saying something moderately wise. What was the matter with her? Of course, this meant that Jamie had to come up with something to equal it.

"We must wait on God's timing," he said solemnly

from time to time. He'd heard a lot of spiritual types say that; it was vague enough to be either meaningless or profound, and could be used in any context. Mary had noticed their competition and gave him an amused side-eye; yeah, that was a good one. Jamie grinned. He was pretty sure he was winning, though he didn't know how long he could keep it up. If only they would go to bed!

Eventually the meal was done, and – much later – the conversation was too. Well, not exactly done, but they realised they'd got into a loop of saying the same things without becoming any wiser on the subject. It's always best to stop when you get to that point, though not everybody can.

The guests began to stand, so the hosts and their lodger stood too. Jamie's eyes had closed and his head was about to loll, dribbling, onto his chest – which would have lost him honour forever in his battles with Miriam – when Mary gave him a nudge.

"We must wait – oh," he said, as his head shot up and he saw what was happening. He got the goodnight hug on offer from Mary to him and Miriam, as the visitors started wrapping shawls and cloaks around themselves and heading to the door.

Then, as if it had been a committee meeting and an invisible chairperson threw in "Any other business?" Eli remembered something which had filled his thoughts before the whole Zechariah thing took him off topic.

"Oh! Joseph – I meant to say – would you and Jamie like to join our group for the walk home? It would be good – to – to – "

He was going to say "to have another man around", but that was clearly nonsense, since he was positively tripping over all his hefty grown-up sons. Good for Joseph to have other guys around? That might sound insulting; Joseph was clearly capable of getting his young boy to and from Jerusalem safely, and if he was happy in his own company, Eli didn't like to suggest his family would be an improvement. So, since Eli couldn't say the *real* reason he thought it would be good, he just repeated lamely "It would be good."

As Joseph also thought it would be extremely good, no discussion was needed and it was agreed more quickly than any committee would. Mary said a hasty goodbye and dashed out to avoid the Very Significant Looks being stifled all round, as everyone tried to pretend that nothing important had just happened. And Jamie, who was blissfully unaware that anything important *had* just happened, also said goodnight and climbed the ladder to their upper room, wondering why Miriam was rolling her eyes at his lack of perception.

Next morning, they went to the Temple to make one last offering; Joseph always did that, as if he couldn't tear himself away – then they met up with their friends.

Sharing the long journey home to Nazareth worked amazingly well, with crossing the river a real high point. It was fun anyway, to hitch your robes up to your knees and wade across, but Jamie had always been a little sad to see other boys having water fights while he was alone. Now, however, he and Clop had an epic battle with each other, and then together attacked Mary's other brothers – a war they could never hope to win, unless the concept of 'winning' a water fight means to end up drenched from head to foot, in which case they were triumphantly victorious.

The women had modestly gone further downstream so that the men didn't see their legs, but Jamie was pleased that they also seemed to be having fun. He could hear their squeals at the coldness of the water, and shrieks of laughter as they splashed each other.

As they walked, they kept pace with each other better than could have been expected. Eli's family were longer in the leg and sturdier in the bladder than Jamie, but they were happy to slow down so he wasn't struggling – and Jamie found he could often go faster than usual, as he was excited to be in a larger group. But it was strange how, even though they were suiting each other so well, most of the time people were not in exactly the same place as Mary, Joseph and Jamie. The three of them tended to be walking together, with the others in their group just slightly ahead or slightly behind.

Jamie was particularly pleased at how quick Mary was to pick up his versions of the Songs of Ascent, which (of course) he had insisted on teaching her. She got the moves down pretty soon and threw herself into the low or high voices, in spite of the jokey comments called out by her brothers further back. She even came up with a good action for Jamie's favourite line:

"'Jerusalem is built like a city – '
(Duh. That's because it is one)"

Mary's idea was to do a big shrug on 'Duh' using the whole of your arms right to your fingertips, then waddle forwards with your feet turned out. We'd call it a penguin walk, but you don't get many penguins at the tonsil end of the Mediterranean, so they had never seen one. They just thought it was a funny walk.

Jamie approved of how seriously she was taking it. Her suggestions were great improvements, which Jamie felt sure would raise the routine to a higher level. He hoped Mary would stick around so they could always travel with her, because the journey really did work much better with three.

Thinking about them being three gave him an idea.

"Will you swing me? Dad used to do that with my mother when I was little."

"No, Jamie... " Joseph cut in quickly.

Mary shot him a look – was he upset at the memory, or just embarrassed that Jamie was asking her to do it? Probably a bit of both, but mainly he was squirming at the assumption Jamie was making in seeing them so clearly as a unit of three, when Mary might not.

"Why?" protested Jamie, determined to be swung.

"You're a lot heavier than you were," was all Joseph would say.

"It's fine," said Mary, and Joseph saw in her eyes that it really was fine.

Jamie took their hands and soon they got the timing exactly right – three quick steps and a long swiiiiiiiing, with Mary and Joseph running perfectly in sync, and then a landing. Mary's parents glanced back and saw what looked very much like a family unit of three.

So Jamie swung along the road to Nazareth to his heart's content, and – way over Jamie's head – Joseph and Mary smiled at each other.

Chapter Seven

THE END (NOT)

Joseph and Jamie were busy once they got home. There were carpentry jobs that had turned up too late to start before they left, and new orders coming in now everyone was back, so they were playing catch-up. Jamie enjoyed helping in the workshop. It was proof to him that he was indeed a big boy, now that he was six. (Bless! I bet you and I thought that when we were six) Going to school *and* becoming a carpenter! In truth, the simple things Joseph was teaching him were not much greater than when he used to play with the wood shavings, making little figures to entertain himself. With no one else to look after him, Jamie had always hung around as his father worked, but he felt very important now he was learning the trade himself.

He also felt important when he went back to the synagogue school, something that had never happened before. The boys went there until they turned thirteen, and as Jamie was among the youngest, he had always felt a bit lost. Not this time, however! Oh no. He was sitting next to his new friend Clop, and they had the inside scoop on the recent event. A few of the boys had been there when Zechariah did his disappearing act, and the others had heard about it when their dads got home. Rabbi Asher had certainly been in the crowd. Probably near the back, Jamie thought to himself with a smirk. The boys wanted to know from their rabbi exactly what had happened, and what it meant.

"The priest was a long time coming out," began Rabbi Asher.

"Zechariah," murmured Jamie – as if commenting to himself, but making sure it was loud enough for everyone to hear.

"What?" snapped Asher, irritated by the interruption.

"The priest's name is Zechariah. His wife's related to Clop."

"Yeah," said Clop, realising what a good game this would be. "We had a fellowship meal with him, and chatted loads."

"Nearly every day," said Jamie, innocently.

Rabbi Asher stared hard at them, wondering if he could deny it. Or top it. He couldn't.

"He's very nice," added Jamie, wondering how far he could push it.

The rabbi turned back to address the whole class with dignity. "The priest had been taken ill in the Holy Place. He seemed to have recovered afterwards, except that sadly he has lost the power of speech. It happens sometimes, at that age."

"He saw a vision," said Jamie, determined that the best bit should not be lost.

"We don't know that," said Asher, picking out a scroll in attempt to move on.

"We do," said Jamie confidently. "He was talking with his hands. Something big and amazing and scary, but something that made him very happy."

"Visions and miracles don't happen, not even to priests," said Asher, unrolling the scroll, determined to get back control of the class.

"Why?" asked Jamie in surprise. "Has God forgotten how?"

"Don't be silly, James," said the rabbi. "Our reading is – " He came to an abrupt halt as he realised which scroll he'd grabbed in his haste to shut Jamie up. "Erm... Ezekiel. The – the vision of the four living creatures and the shining man. Begin."

Boom; first round to Jamie. The bigger boys took notice of him now. He never tired of answering questions about what Zechariah was like, everything he'd ever said to Jamie, and what gestures he had made while Jamie was looking after him. Jamie got his impersonation slickly polished, and had many requests for the startling alien-who-had-popped-out-for-chips-and-found-himself-on-earth moment: clinging faintly to a door post, then staggering towards his awestruck schoolmates with arms stretched out and eyes rolling. Every time Jamie performed it, his enactment became more gruesome, bigger than Clop's version and less like the real event. All in all, it was much less boring than the usual return to Nazareth.

Then one day Jamie was surprised to see Joseph with the bright red lobster-look. Why had he had a bath, and why was he in fresh clothes? It wasn't Shabbat, the day of rest they took once a week. Joseph looked scrubbed up for a jaunt somewhere special, not an ordinary working day in a monotonously-beyond-ordinary town.

"Jamie," said Joseph. Rather formal – and a little pointless, as there was no one else there. "I'm going to Eli's house."

Jamie brightened. He'd been looking forward to when they would have time to visit, but he knew that, as a craftsman now, work must come first.

"I'll come with you," he said.

"No," said Joseph, surprisingly nervous. "I'm sorry. It's important."

Ah, this sounded like business.

"Do they want a table, or a door?" asked Jamie. "I could help you measure."

"No," repeated Joseph – the word he seemed to feel safest with just now. "It's something I need to do by myself. Our neighbour will look after you."

Jamie crinkled his nose. He'd been looked after by her before. She was always too busy to take notice of him, and she didn't know how to bake yummy things like Dinah did.

"I'll go to one of Mary's brothers' houses," said Jamie, thinking of the fussing and petting and fun tricks they would teach him.

"No," said Joseph, thinking of the teasing and laughing and Very Significant Looks. "Come on, I'll drop you round."

Sometimes – often – Joseph could be persuaded if it would make Jamie happy, and sometimes he couldn't; this was clearly one of the latter. Jamie could not have made his nose crinklier or his frown glummer, but round he was dropped at the neighbour's regardless. And what an age it was before Joseph returned! Their neighbour swept her whole house, by which time the dust had settled back down in the first part, so she swept it again – and then again! Jamie sat on a step and watched mesmerised, as if his life had gone into a loop and he would never get out until he crumbled into dust and got swept away himself. She never asked how he was, or if he was hungry or thirsty (though he guessed there must be a film of dust on everything, so the idea wasn't that appetising). He knew instinctively she wouldn't be interested in his famous portrayal of Zechariah coming out of the Temple.

Finally, Joseph appeared and took his hand to lead him home without a word, nodding his thanks to the neighbour as they left.

Back home he sat Jamie on a little stool and faced him, clearing his throat as if about to deliver a lecture. Visiting Eli's house had apparently not made him any less nervous.

"Jamie," he started, again with no one else there. "The thing is... "

Jamie watched him struggle to find more words. Ideally, ones that might fit into some kind of a sentence and possibly even have a recognisable meaning. Jamie decided to help him out.

"Did you have a nice time?"

"Yes," said Joseph. "The thing is... "

"Was Mary there?"

"Yes." Joseph swallowed hard. Even the few words he'd gathered for this tricky conversation seemed to be escaping from his head and running off to play.

"You should marry her," said Jamie.

"The thing is, Jamie – I – what?" Joseph stared at him astounded – with every word or phrase he had ever known, from his very first utterance ('tea towel') to the most recent he had heard ('entomology'), waving goodbye and dancing into the sunset.

"Mary," said Jamie. "You should marry her. Then she could look after me when you have to go out, and we could make up more songs. And she could come and live at our house, so we wouldn't have to go to Eli's to see her."

Joseph knew he was staring at Jamie boggle-eyed. He managed to grab back a few useful words and somehow string them together.

"Yes. Wouldn't you not be not upset? Would you would like that if?"

"I'd like it a lot," said Jamie, not noticing his father's unusual turn of phrase; he sometimes struggled with complicated ideas himself. "I'd specially like it if Dinah tells her how to make my favourite cakes."

"I'm... sure that could be managed," said Joseph, relieved to be thinking in proper sentences again. "Well – that's a very good idea, Jamie. Right. I'll do that. I'll marry Mary." He kneeled in front of Jamie's little stool. "Remember, though; you don't ever need to be jealous."

Jamie was surprised. Why would he be jealous?

"We might have children, God willing," explained Joseph. "Brothers and sisters for you. But you'd know I still loved you just as much, wouldn't you?"

Jamie's eyes narrowed, considering. He'd seen small children; those little wrigglers could be demanding, which would be inconvenient if they were doing it at a time when Jamie wanted to be demanding himself. He thought it through carefully: lots of younger children, all looking up to him and thinking how clever he was. Yes; Jamie decided he could make it work.

"As long as they know I'm the oldest," he said with satisfaction.

So it was arranged that Joseph and Mary would get engaged, and the next thing to do was have a big party. You don't need me to tell you how beautiful Mary looked, or that Joseph was very handsome and well turned out. I probably don't need to mention that most of the small town came along to wish them joy. You'll certainly already be aware that both Jamie and Clop ate way more cakes than was good for them, yet somehow managed to keep piling them in without chucking up.

It was wonderful for Jamie, to be right at the centre of an important event in Nazareth. Eli's family was large and well known in the town, and now Jamie was going to belong to it! No more just Joseph and Jamie. All of that boisterous clan took the father and son to their heart, and Jamie was loving it. The only annoying thing was that nobody believed him when he said this engagement was all his idea. Whenever he tried to explain that, people just laughed and ruffled his hair.

This party changed everything and made the new relationship official and very public. No more hidden laughs and whispered teasing – all the laughter was out in the open and bursting with happiness.

In that culture, a betrothal was much more than simply telling your family and friends you were going to get married and showing the ring. It was as legally binding as a wedding! Joseph and Mary stood with Rabbi Asher in front of everyone and made promises to God that they would marry, and lots of people cried.

Then Clop sneaked up behind Joseph and pinned a sign on him saying 'Just Betrothed' with strings attached to stones, shells and bits of metal that clattered along the ground as he walked, and lots of people laughed. Very sportingly, Joseph kept it on till he got home.

The only difference between a betrothal and the actual marriage was that the bride-to-be did not yet move in with the groom. He would now prepare a home for her, and only when everything was ready would he come to collect her and they would have a big wedding feast – doubtless with a ton of cake.

The groom's parents would usually give him a patch of land and he would build a house – or at least an extra room attached to his parents' house. Joseph already had his own home, of course, but it was dingy and mostly taken up with his carpentry gear. He had grand plans to make it nice for Mary – comfy and spacious, with the workshop in a separate room, and ornamental carving on the doors and window shutters. Joseph had many grand plans for his new life with Mary.

An engagement party, and high hopes for the future – what a perfect end to the story! Thank you so much for reading; it's been lovely.

Certainly, that's the end of those soppy romances some people are so fond of, and pretty much every fairy tale too. The couple whom we and all their friends just knew were right for each other and should get together, *have* got together. What more is there for me to say, except that Jamie finally got the recognition he deserved as a prince, Miriam founded Jerusalem's first university at the age of ten and they all lived happily ever after.

But I promised you this was not going to be a fairy tale – plus, if we leave it here, it would be a rather short book and you'd probably be contacting the place you bought it and demanding your money back, or writing huffy reviews on bookish websites. Nor would I blame you. Even worse, if you have an eye for story structure, as I hope you do, you would be wondering why I bothered telling you about the Curious Incident of the Priest in the Temple, if I was never going to explain what actually happened.

So – you *can* finish here, if you really want to. Bye.

But you know full well that there was far more in store for Mary and Joseph, don't you? Getting betrothed was just the start of their adventure.

Chapter Eight

AND HE WILL BE CALLED – SORRY, WHAT?

Still here? Good.

Besides their connection to Eli's family, the recent trip to Jerusalem had produced a curiosity in Jamie about this Anointed One they were waiting for, which lasted longer than any extra chubbiness from Dinah's cooking. When he was at the rabbi's school, he started noticing bits of the Holy Writings that might be about this special descendant of King David, who was somehow going to save his people *and* their enemies at the same time. That would be a stunt way beyond any magician in the Temple courts, if he managed it.

The prophet called Isaiah seemed to have a good take on the subject, so Jamie tried to concentrate when they were looking at one of his scrolls, and not let his mind wander onto what kind of crown he would like when he was declared a prince, or how long you could live on nothing but honey before your teeth fell out.

Isaiah had the bits the rabbi was fond of, with the Saviour stomping about on his enemies, like squashing grapes. But Anna was right that it seemed to be about saving as much as squashing. And who was this Saviour, anyway? It said God himself would have to do the saving, because there wasn't anyone else.

One particular day grabbed Jamie's attention, when Clop stood at the front of the synagogue and read out a passage in Hebrew, then translated it for everyone:

"'The Spirit of the... kingish...'"

"Sovereign," prompted Rabbi Asher.

Clop tried again: "'The Spirit of the Sovereign Lord is on the top of my head, –'"

"Just 'upon me' will do," said Asher.

"Oh yeah," said Clop. "'Because the Lord has oil-dribbled me – anointed me – to tell happy news to poor people. He has sent me to bandage smashed hearts, to shout "FREEDOM!!!" at captive people – '"

"To proclaim freedom *for* the captives," corrected Asher with his resting irritated face.

Jamie listened carefully; bandaging smashed hearts and cheering up poor people didn't sound much like a warrior waving a sword. He would have to put the sword down to do any serious bandaging, for a start.

"To proclaim freedom for captive people and a getting-out-of-darkness for prisoners," continued Clop. "To shout – To *proclaim* the year of the Lord's niceness... loveliness... *favour*... and the day of revenge of our God."

Aha! Revenge would certainly need a sword. Yet Jamie noticed it was a whole year of niceness and only one day of revenge. And against whom would the sword be waving? Isaiah didn't say.

Clop went back to his place, and Rabbi Asher sat on the floor in front of the loose semicircle of boys.

"Not bad in parts, I suppose. But this is a famous section; you shouldn't still be struggling, Cleopas. Make an effort to learn it for next time."

"Yes, Rabbi," said Clop's mouth, while his facial expression clearly said "Not a chance, Rabbi."

"Who is God going to take revenge on?" butted in Jamie, anxious to cut to the chase. The other boys glanced at each other, amused by such a simple question. You'd have to be almost a toddler not to have learned that yet.

"Our enemy, obviously – the Romans," explained Rabbi Asher dismissively. "Isaiah is – "

"Why?" asked Jamie.

"Why? Because they are our oppressors!" exploded Asher. "Haven't you been listening? We are the captives, and Messiah – the one who is anointed by God

– will set us free."

"From darkness, or from Romans?" frowned Jamie, trying to grasp it.

"From the darkness of Roman rule. Isaiah is – "

"What about the bit we did about him lighting up Gentiles?" asked Jamie. "It said *they* were sitting in the dark. If the Romans got lit up, we would have peace."

"He is not going to light up the Romans!" barked Asher with great finality. "That passage must refer to a few Gentiles whom God has deemed worthy. Isaiah – "

"There's something else about peace, and a baby," said Tolomai, Clop's friend, fired up by what Jamie was saying and grabbing the scroll. "Give it here, Clop. It's near that bit about him lighting up Gentiles."

"It says the Gentiles will *see* a great light; the light will *dawn* on them – it doesn't say he'll light *them* up," protested the rabbi weakly, but control of the lesson had long since slipped through his grasp.

"Here it is," said Tolomai, as the other boys shuffled over on their bottoms to look. "'The Lord himself will give you a sign: the virgin will be pregnant, and will have a son, and people will call him Immanuel.'"

"Means 'God with us'," Clop translated for the young ones, suddenly interested now they'd taken over.

"What's a virgin?" asked Jamie.

The other boys stifled giggles.

"Not necessarily 'virgin'," jumped in Rabbi Asher, determined not to go there. "The Hebrew word can also be translated 'young woman'. It refers to Isaiah's wife."

"Then how is it a sign?" asked Jamie, unconvinced. Signs from God were supposed to be *amazing*, to make people sit up and take notice – whereas young women were always having babies, from what Jamie had seen. Some of them never seemed to do anything else. In fact, if you had to guess what type of person in the whole world was the most likely to have a baby, surely it would be a young woman? If that was all it meant, it didn't seem to be one of Isaiah's greatest hits:

"Guys, guys – you'll never guess! God's just said who's going to have a baby! You won't believe it! It's a *young woman!!!*"

His friends would probably have told him to have a lie down, and maybe not write that one in his book.

"The rabbi we used to have said it was one of those double fulfilments," said Tolomai.

"Did he," muttered Asher, wishing *that* rabbi had stuck around to field all the questions.

"Yeah," said Tolomai, skimming down the scroll. "It meant that some stuff would happen when Isaiah's wife had a baby, but there's another, future baby thing just after. Here, look. The Gentiles will light up, – "

"They'll be in Galilee!" shouted Clop, crashing his head against Tolomai's as he tried to read the scroll with him. "The lit-up Gentiles'll be here in Galilee! Cool."

"Sticks that oppressed us will be broken," said Tolomai, rubbing his head and trying to shove Clop out of the way, desperate to make his point. "And there'll be a bonfire of warriors' boots. No more tyranny, because – "

"'To us a child is born, to us a son is given!'" interrupted Clop, nearly falling on to the scroll in his enthusiasm to be the one to translate it. "'And the government will be on the top of his shoulders. And he will be called... Mind-blowing Psychotherapist – '"

"'Wonderful Counsellor,'" corrected Tolomai, barging Clop sideways to the floor so he could see the scroll himself. "'Mighty God, Everlasting Father, Prince of *Peace*. His government and *peace* will never stop growing. And he will sit on David's throne, blah blah blah, forever.'"

Tolomai looked at Rabbi Asher with shining eyes, sure he would be delighted with his knowledge of the scriptures. "See? That's not Mrs Isaiah's baby – that's

Messiah, in't it, Rabbi? And we'll have peace and he'll be our king, but we won't need warrior boots 'cos we won't have to fight the Romans to get it."

"So, what's a virgin?" persisted Jamie, determined to understand it – both the Messiah stuff and why the other boys kept sniggering every time he said that word.

"Oh, for goodness sake, James," sighed the rabbi in despair. "I shouldn't have to explain this to you. Has your father ever had a little conversation with you about how babies... come to be?"

Jamie cast his mind back. There had been something. It had started with how the mummy and the daddy loved each other very much, and then it had all got a bit technical.

"I think so," he said, cautiously non-committal.

"Well," said Asher, clearing his throat more than seemed necessary, "a virgin is someone who has never – done anything that could make a baby."

That was more like it! In the miraculous sign department, Jamie felt that for one of these virgins to have a baby was definitely of more God-like proportions than yet another young woman. That was something that would grab attention big time.

"Isaiah is – " Rabbi Asher continued and broke off, seeing parents gathering to collect the younger boys, signalling the end of the lesson. "The Lord be praised," he muttered, grabbing the scroll and taking it to where they were stored so that no one else could talk to him. Ever again, if possible. From now on he resolved to cover nothing but lists, counting and measuring things. There was plenty of that in the scrolls; it should take him happily through to retirement. The boys were so much easier to teach when they were bored.

Jamie chewed over what he was finding out. The stomping, swords and being a great soldier was only for one day, and the niceness, bandaging hearts and saving people seemed to last much longer. Jamie decided that must be because the Anointed One would be so good at fighting, the battle with the Romans would be short. He just hoped he would get a chance to join in. Maybe he could introduce himself, and say that he was descended from King David too, so they were related! Messiah might let Jamie fight next to him, and give him a crown so everyone would know that Jamie was practically a prince. But the important thing was simple: for their Saviour to reign on David's throne blah blah blah forever, like Tolomai had quoted, he would have to kick out Herod and the Romans. The prophets who wrote about *all* nations being blessed through him must have forgotten to put 'except the Romans, or anyone else who is mean to us.' Anna's idea of the Anointed One coming to save everybody at the same time didn't make sense.

The part about the lit-up Gentiles interested Jamie too, especially as it was going to be in Galilee. There were certainly more Gentiles living up here than in Judea, plus traders passing through. Not just people who went to the Temple and tried to pray, but others, with their own gods. If this mighty rescuer they were waiting for was going to be lighting up Gentiles in Galilee, he'd surely have to come near Nazareth to do it? *That* would be Jamie's chance to say hello.

Jamie very much wanted to see the lit-up Gentiles; it would be spectacular! Whatever the rabbi said, he did so hope that a least a few would be lit up, temporarily. Maybe even float around in the sky? He was sure God would be able to do it in a way that didn't hurt them.

Chapter Nine

SEASONS OF JOY

Joseph and Jamie set off early to the next week-long festival in Jerusalem, to work on the small room on Miriam's roof. Joseph wanted to patch it up and make a proper staircase for when he brought Mary there after they were married. Jamie was disappointed that this meant Mary, Eli and the rest didn't travel with them, but at least they came to wave them off. Mary gave Jamie a kiss as she promised she'd see him there soon, and Joseph told him he was very lucky to be getting kisses from Mary. Mary blushed a little and laughed a little, retreating to the safety of her sisters in case there was another outbreak of teasing. In that culture there would be no kissing for the betrothed couple until they were married.

One good thing about arriving ahead of everyone else – apart from dodging the crowds – was that they got to tell their incredible news about the betrothal without Eli's family there, trying to tell it too.

Miriam, Dinah and Matthan didn't look too surprised. Pleased, yes, but with considerable lack of amazement. Jamie thought they mustn't have understood properly, so as Matthan took Joseph to pour him a congratulatory drink, he explained it again to Miriam and Dinah, including how it had all been his idea.

"Everyone knew. It was obvious," scoffed Miriam as she went to iron some hankies, or whatever she did with her free time.

"It *was* my idea," Jamie protested to Dinah. "I thought of it, and I told Dad he should marry Mary!"

"It doesn't matter how many people get the same idea," said Dinah, giving him a cuddle. "It doesn't stop it being a good one. I bet your dad was happier than you can imagine when you came up with it."

As they ate together, Jamie and Joseph were keen to hear what had happened with Zechariah and Elizabeth.

"She stayed here, then Dad and me dropped them back home," said Miriam. "Zechariah still couldn't talk. He just kept squeezing her hand and kissing it."

"He's back for the festivals," added Matthan; "I saw him yesterday. I called to him but he was too far away. I wanted to ask if Elizabeth would like to stay again."

Another good thing about showing up early was that they could go to a mini celebration they usually missed: the Festival of Trumpets, which was exactly what it sounds like. (It was even better in Hebrew! 'Yom Teruah' – 'Day of Shouting') The priests made an unimaginable din on rams' horns and silver trumpets, and everyone gave a mighty yell. Anyone today who thinks worship can only mean quiet contemplation with no place for drums or bass would have got quite a shock if they'd rocked up at the Temple two thousand years ago. They hadn't even invented ear plugs yet. It was Jamie's first time and he thought it was one of God's most tremendous ideas, without having a clue why they were doing it. Cast your mind back to when you were six; if you ask one of those little fellas to be as noisy as they can, the finer spiritual points may get lost.

Then they got down to making the upper room nice. The skilled work fell to Joseph, of course. Jamie did much of the sanding, and showed Miriam how to work along the grain so as not to scratch the beauty of the wood. Matthan's thing was the carrying, and holding heavy pieces in place as Joseph lined them up. Dinah was great at both carrying and hammering, but needed sometimes to take time out for her other superpower – cooking – which they all insisted was every bit as important if the work was to continue apace.

They were on track until the interruption of another ceremony, to Jamie's frustration; he didn't think this one was anywhere near as good an idea as shouting. The Day of Atonement was the one day of the year when the high priest was allowed into the final onion ring humans could enter, known as the Most Holy Place. In the old days, before it was lost, he would have seen the last onion ring of all: the Ark of the Covenant, a golden chest which *no one* could ever look in.

While all the other holy days involved feasting, this was a fast. Jamie had a difficult choice. Small children were allowed to eat, so Dinah offered him breakfast, but that would mean publicly admitting he wasn't such a big boy as he liked to think. He decided to refuse breakfast in a noble and solemn way, then eat it quickly once Miriam wasn't looking. He also made sure Dinah had secret snacks ready for later. Miriam, of course, seemed ready to live on thin air until sunset – but she hadn't been forced to follow the complicated Hebrew reading Joseph had insisted on doing on the roof as soon as they woke, which would make anyone hungry.

Joseph and Matthan went to the Temple while Dinah and the children stayed at home. They spent the time quietly, with Miriam thinking about God and Jamie thinking about how he could get at his hidden stash of food without her seeing.

Next morning it was back to the frenzied sawing, hammering and sanding. They only had two more days till Mary arrived! True, she was not going to be moving in right now, but Joseph and Jamie were keen it should be the best it could when they showed it to her.

And so it was, and Mary was delighted. She went up and down the stairs several times – sometimes holding on to the special handrail and sometimes not – and expressed how wide and smooth they were, how easy to use, and what a good idea the covered walkway was, that took you across the flat roof to the room itself. Jamie showed her what he had done, and she marvelled. She didn't even notice the places in the upper room where there had been holes, because Joseph had mended them so cleverly. Everybody thought, but only Dinah was bold enough to say, that they looked forward to the next time she would visit, when they would welcome her as a bride and she would stay here with them.

Now things were really hotting up as everyone prepared for the next celebration. Eli's family were suddenly everywhere, and Jamie couldn't wait to share with them what had to be the most fun of all the festivals – more fun *even* than shouting. Imagine if an entire nation decided to have one massive sleepover together: *that* was the Feast of Tabernacles.

It was another Harvest Festival, this time because the fruit crop was safely gathered in: apples, oranges, figs, dates, melons, anagrams of melons (lemons) and, most important in that land, olives and grapes (yes, olives are a fruit. Don't try putting them in fruit salads; people won't thank you).

But it was so much more than just a Harvest Festival! It remembered how the people of Israel had lived in tents in the wilderness after they escaped from slavery in Egypt – *and* it remembered how the presence of God himself had come down to live in a tent like a glorious cloud, so he could be with them: the richly embroidered Tabernacle, long before the Temple was built.

This meant that everyone was going to live outdoors, in shelters or booths they built from leafy branches and palm fronds, decorated with any fruit they could find. It was all the excitement and anticipation of decorating a Christmas tree, if you've ever done that, but taken up so many more levels because you were actually going to *live* in it, like a super-special tree house. Of course, many of the B&B / hotel / Jerusalem-resident people cheated by building a shelter attached to their house, but it was still good fun. And the diehard campers had the most amazing time on the hills around Jerusalem, with games, torchlight, barbeques, and singsongs going late into the night.

Jamie and Joseph had always built their shelter on the roof, with Miriam and her parents in one next to them, so that it was hardly any different from sleeping in the upper room. This time, however – oh, *this* time, they were going all-out ninja camping, as Eli had invited the five to join his ever-extending family. They spent a whole day building their shelters, gathered around a rough square so they had space in the middle to chill together, outdoing each other with the leafiness and fruitiness of their decorations. It was the best time *ever*. Jamie couldn't contain his excitement, making little squeaks like a smoke alarm when its battery runs down; Clop managed to strand himself up a tree, and even Miriam was caught hopping with glee when she found a wild pomegranate with orange-pink fruit too hidden away to have been harvested. Joining in with everyone was unbelievably cool, plus Miriam and Jamie were snug in the knowledge that they could have the best of both worlds and nip back for home comforts or dry clothes any time they liked.

They went to the Temple, of course, to do the feast properly – and, my – 'properly' was not the word! There were more instructions to rejoice for this festival than any other. So much so, it was actually known as the Season of our Joy! And the Hebrew word for 'rejoice' does not just mean smile occasionally, or put a paper hat on while you have your dinner; the literal translation means to bounce around crazily, so that is what they did. Every day there was shouting at dawn as they turned together to face the Temple; there was a torchlight procession around the streets at midnight, and a psalm-singing procession in the middle of the day when they all played musical instruments – regardless of whether or not they knew how – and danced together up the wide Temple steps.

On one of the Temple visits, Jamie spotted Anna in the Court of Women. Rather than sitting propped up against a pillar praying quietly, she was active and energised, still pacing and muttering just as when they had last seen her. Jamie wondered if she was upset or worried about something, but as he watched he saw it was more a pent-up excitement. Expectancy, that was it; Anna was expecting something to happen. It gave Jamie a fluttery tummy, although he didn't know what the anticipated thing might be. He noticed that she was looking around a lot, staring at people, especially young women, with her laser-like, penetrating eyes. What was she looking for? Had she seen it yet?

Dinah gave Jamie and Miriam some food to give her, and Anna smiled and ate it without any of her usual tucking it away and forgetting about it. Whereas before, Jamie always used to feel she'd be happy to slip away, he now had the idea that she firmly intended to stick around. She clearly wasn't going anywhere until the thing she was looking forward to happened.

Mary came over to tell them that their group had found a corner to sit in. She smiled her pure, bright smile at Anna as she took the children's hands, and Anna's eyes locked onto hers. If Jamie had happened to glance back as Mary led them away, he would have seen that Anna was no longer looking here and there throughout the crowd. No, not at all. She stood completely still, watching Mary until she disappeared from her sight.

Chapter Ten

THE RUNAWAY BRIDE

They wanted to check that Zechariah was all right while they were in Jerusalem, but he was tricky to get hold of, mostly staying near the Temple building – closer than they were allowed go – kneeling or standing alone in front of it. He did wander by at one point and Eli tried to speak to him, but it was hard to know if he couldn't hear or just wasn't interested after whatever he had seen in the Holy Place.

"I wish we knew how they were!" fretted Eli. "Where is Elizabeth? She never misses the feasts."

"There's Rabbi Reuben, one of their neighbours," said Miriam, pointing at a man sitting in a quiet corner, teaching a small group of his followers. "We met him when we took them home."

"Did you really?" asked Eli. They went over eagerly.

The rabbi interrupted his lecture to stand and greet them. Eli explained their concerns, but Reuben didn't have much to tell other than that they seemed fine.

"I haven't really seen Elizabeth the last three or four months," he said. "She doesn't go out now."

"What, ever?" exclaimed Eli. "Oh, poor Elizabeth! I wonder if my wife and I should go to look after her?"

"We'll care for them if they need it," the rabbi assured him. "But the one time I did catch a glimpse of her, she looked very well. Blooming, in fact."

"But you say she's staying in the house all the time," persisted Eli. "And Zechariah still can't speak!"

"I know," said Rabbi Reuben, patiently trying to get it through to him; "but they don't seem ill."

They had to be content with that, as the next day was the final day of the feast, Shemini Atzeret, focused on the fulfilment of the law God had given them and a new beginning. Then it was their usual early morning goodbye offering, and time to return to Nazareth. Inspired by the all-singing, all-dancing processions of the feast, Mary and Jamie picked another Song of Ascent to make up their own version:

"'How good and pleasant it is – '
(Oooh, yes – it's very nice)
' – when God's people live together in unity!'
(That's a feeling, not a place)
'It is like precious oil poured on the head – '
(Perfumed oil, not cooking oil. Ew, that'd be yuk)
'Running down on the beard – '
(Not mine, 'cos I don't have one)
'Running down on *Aaron's* beard – '
(Glug glug glug)... "

– you get the idea. It was in pretty good shape by the time they got home, with actions and everything. Joseph managed to get away without joining in much. He was happy to let Mary have all Jamie's attention, and took advantage of the most peaceful journey he'd had for three or four years.

Not that the song and dance routine lasted the *whole* of the long walk, of course. Jamie demanded to be swung from time to time, and there was also plenty of chance to talk about their plans. Joseph felt that their soon-to-be home together was likely to be up to even his high standards within a couple of months, and they agreed how wonderful it would be for Joseph and Mary to marry at Hanukkah – a celebration of light in the dark, wet winter.

With that hope spurring them on, Joseph and Jamie worked flat out when they got back, and they fixed a day during the celebrations when Joseph would marry her and bring her home. Jamie couldn't believe that at last he would have a mother in the house at Hanukkah, to light the pretty candles and say the special prayers each night. Mary was full of joy, getting more and more beautiful as the wedding drew near. She even let Jamie see the dress she was going to wear. The wedding day was so close Jamie felt he could touch it as easily as he let the embroidered linen robe run through his fingers.

And then something went wrong.

At least – Jamie thought it must have gone wrong, but he simply didn't know. No one did. The first clue was when he ran to Eli's house just a few days before the wedding to recite for Mary the little Hebrew blessing he had pestered Clop and Tolomai to teach him. He was going to say it over the happy couple during the ceremony. It was supposed to be a surprise, but Jamie couldn't wait and thought she might as well have the surprise now.

Mary was alone and very distracted, as if she'd had a shock. As if she were trying to process something, but it was simply too much. Jamie looked around carefully. He didn't want other people to hear the special secret.

"Is anybody else here?" he asked, and Mary swung around startled, as if somebody might have suddenly appeared from nowhere behind her.

She calmed down, seeing they hadn't. "No. No, they all went out. I was just starting the dinner."

She didn't look like someone starting the dinner, as she clasped and unclasped her hands, her thoughts darting around. Jamie explained that he had learned something especially for the wedding, but she wasn't listening, which was not like her at all. She suddenly crouched down in front of him and seized his hands, looking earnestly into his face.

"I love you, Jamie," she said. "And I love your father very much. You know that, don't you?"

"Yes, of course," said Jamie, wide-eyed in wonder.

71

Mary looked so serious but then she suddenly laughed, her face all lit up just as Zechariah's had been with that strange, unspeakable joy.

Then she hugged Jamie – no, she *clung* to him, and gave him one of her precious kisses – and then she pushed him gently to the door!

"You'd better go. Goodbye. Remember I love you."

And, somehow, he was back out in the street with the door shut in front of him, without quite knowing how it had happened.

Jamie didn't know whether to tell his father. He didn't want to worry him, but it did seem so very odd that he felt they should do something. He was glad when, not long after, Joseph said he was going to see Eli to sort the final arrangements. Joseph said Jamie would be bored and was going to drop him at one of Mary's brothers, but Jamie was the most grown up he had ever been as he insisted on going with him.

Eli looked worried. At first it didn't seem he was even going to let them in, which was unthinkable of such a hospitable man and a friend so close he'd become like a father to Joseph. But then he thought twice and held the door open, trying to give a smile of welcome.

"Hello – yes. Come in, come in!" he said awkwardly as they entered, both looking around for Mary, though for very different reasons. "I'm afraid Mary isn't here. She's gone out." He hesitated, knowing that wouldn't do but finding it very hard to say what he needed. "She's gone away. Gone. Yes, that's it. Mary has gone."

Gone? Joseph stared at him. It was a simple word, but he couldn't even begin to understand it.

Eli cleared his throat and fiddled with his hands. "She said she was going to stay with Elizabeth."

Oh, that made sense; Joseph brightened with relief.

"You must have had word from them. Is Elizabeth ill – or Zechariah? I suppose a few of your family are

72

making the journey."

"No, no. We've heard nothing. She's gone alone. She just said she was going to stay with Elizabeth."

There was a silence as Joseph took it in. Travelling alone. A long journey. In winter. A couple of days before their wedding. Without telling him, or saying goodbye. Without giving any reason. Mary had gone.

Jamie looked up at his father, seeing the pain in his eyes. "Mary loves you," he whispered.

"Oh, she does, Joseph!" exclaimed Eli, nearly in tears. "I'm sure she loves you. I don't understand it."

"The wedding," Joseph managed to say.

"Yes, I know. We'll have to tell people that it's – postponed."

There was another pause, in which the word 'cancelled' hung heavily without anyone saying it.

Joseph nodded a brief goodbye to Eli and led Jamie to the door.

"Tell us if you hear from her," he said, and they went back to their home – so nice and comfortable now, but doubly empty as the person it had been made nice for had gone.

Mary must be so brave, thought Jamie. He didn't know why she had done it, but just the thought of her travelling for days on her own, with robbers sometimes wandering the countryside and not many places to find food or shelter – he couldn't imagine how much courage it would take. It must be something very important for her to go all that way alone, when he had seen how much she wanted to stay here and marry Joseph.

"Maybe it's something to do with God," said Jamie to his father as the two of them got ready to light the first candle for Hanukkah that night. "She's very kind. Maybe God nudged her heart to say that she needs to see Elizabeth. And maybe she felt she needed to go right away."

"Maybe," said Joseph.

And he sparked the flame that symbolised God's miraculous light coming into the darkness.

It was horrible going around the little town with people staring and guessing – and some, such as Rabbi Asher, even asking for detail about why she had gone. Eli tried to make it sound as if she had been summoned urgently, but it didn't fool anyone. Why would her mother, Elizabeth's cousin, not have gone too? Why would some men from the family not have accompanied them for protection? Above all, why would a bride disappear, seemingly alone, two days before her wedding? Quite a few people in Nazareth looked as if it was pretty easy to work out. Whatever – or *who*ever – else may have been involved, she certainly didn't want to marry Joseph.

Eli sent messages south to Judea with passing traders to try to find out what was happening, of course, but all he ever heard back was that Elizabeth, Zechariah and Mary were well and sent their love. So they knew Mary had arrived safely, but that was all. Eli desperately wanted to go there himself, but he knew it would look bad. Chasing after his daughter to bring her back? What would the townsfolk make of that? It would have looked even worse if Joseph had gone after her. Joseph kept a dignified silence when questioned, and Eli continued to bluff it out as if they knew all about it and Mary's journey had been planned, even if nobody believed it. They could do nothing more.

The memory of Mary's radiant face was some comfort to Jamie. Zechariah's joy as he laughed, too; Elizabeth reportedly looking 'blooming', and Anna, up on her feet and unusually active, waiting for something big. Expectancy, that was what was in the air. Strange things were happening, and those four had been disturbed by it more than anyone – yet they didn't seem afraid. Quite the opposite. Jamie took hope; from them, and from the excited, fluttery tummy he got when he thought about it.

Whenever Jamie saw that sad look come into his father's eyes he whispered "Mary loves you," and Joseph nodded.

"I know she does," he sometimes managed to reply.

All there was to do, for both of them, was trust. That is hard when you don't know the reason – but then, if you understood the reason, you wouldn't need to trust. They knew Mary and the sort of person she was, and they knew she loved them. For now, that would have to be enough.

It did get easier as time passed, but they were still thankful as spring approached. Now they would have an excuse to go south without attracting more gossip. Soon it would be the month of Nisan and Pesach, the Passover, the first of the year's great feasts when all Jewish men had to present themselves at the Temple. Hebron was comparatively only a hop and a skip further south of Jerusalem, so they could pay a visit to Elizabeth and Zechariah's house and actually see what was going on.

The plan was to go early to do that, but there was fever in Nazareth; Jamie and several of Eli's family were too ill to travel. Jamie was torn between wanting his father to go without him, to get there as soon as possible to see Mary – and wanting to be there himself so he could hear in person why she had gone. The choice wasn't Jamie's, however. Joseph refused to leave him while he was ill. It was possible he had already lost the woman he loved; there was absolutely no way Joseph was going to risk losing his son.

Once Jamie was well, there was only enough time to make it for Passover itself. No singing on the way, no fun and games with Clop (who was still sneezing green slime across the bedroom), just determined walking to get to the Temple; to get to Mary.

Joseph had sent a message on ahead to Miriam's family, carried by Tolomai's father – a very honest man, and not the kind to judge or spread rumours. Their hosts needed to know that the wedding hadn't happened, or Dinah was likely to deck the place out with flowers to welcome the bride. Joseph and Jamie didn't feel they could cope with seeing their friends' faces as they broke the news.

Chapter Eleven

WHEN JAMIE WAS RIGHT

Jamie and Joseph were very glad they'd sent that message. It was bad enough to arrive with Miriam and her parents already knowing: their looks of confusion and sadness; wanting to ask why but not liking to, in case it caused hurt. And how could Jamie and Joseph tell them that they had no idea why it had happened? Fortunately, when friends really care about you, words are not always needed. The father and son got none of the prying looks or thinly-disguised hints they had been used to, just a load of love and support.

They got to Jerusalem amidst the frenzy of Preparation Day, with just enough time to purify themselves and go to the Temple. Matthan had already chosen a lamb out of the many brought into the city from Bethlehem, a nearby village, where they were bred especially for this day (you know the deal; don't get too attached to this lamb). They stood in line to make the sacrifice, then Dinah cooked it to perfection so that they could eat the very holy feast together that night.

The day after the Passover was a special Sabbath, so no work was allowed. Normally such a rule was a wonderful blessing, as even the harshest employers or keenest teachers could not make people come in or do holiday homework. Ha! But if walking or riding more than a little way counts as work, and if the person you are desperate to see is twenty miles away, it's not something to be pleased about.

Jamie and Joseph coped with the enforced rest as best they could and were all set to go to Hebron early the day after, when they found a message had been slid under the door from Zechariah and Elizabeth themselves. The beautifully written invitation said:

77

'Come and celebrate with us
the safe arrival of our baby son!'

Wait, what – *baby???* An actual *baby???* Elizabeth was – well, I don't mean to be rude, but she wasn't young. She would have collected her free bus pass by now in any modern city that treats its older residents with that kind of respect. If Jamie had, quite rightly, observed that the natural demographic for having babies was young women, then Elizabeth did *not* fall within it. And anyway, hadn't Mary said the couple had never been able to have children? If true, this would be a miracle *almost* as astonishing as one of those virgins having a baby.

They stared at each other open-mouthed and then everyone kept grabbing the invitation off everyone else – even Dinah and Miriam, who had never been taught to read. But there it was, clear as anything:

'Born after sunset on Nisan 14th
weighing 6 minas 12 shekels.
Mother and baby both doing well'

That settled it.

Dinah had felt strongly it would be best if Joseph went to see Mary alone, to give them a chance to talk... but... Elizabeth had had a *baby???* Everyone started piling into sandals, shawls and cloaks, and there was no more talk of discretion.

Matthan borrowed his neighbour's cart again so they could be as speedy as possible, and they were off. Partway to Hebron they overtook some of Mary's family, run-walking and walk-running along the dusty road, nearly falling over each other in their haste.

"Elizabeth – " wheezed Eli.

"We know!" shouted Joseph, hauling them aboard without even stopping.

As Jamie watched everyone's keenness to see this

wonder, a fantastic thought occurred to him.

"This is why Mary came!" he yelled in triumph. "God must have put it in her head. She guessed it somehow, and she rushed to be with Elizabeth – just like we are now!"

Everyone was amazed at the idea. Could God have hinted it to her somehow?

"I don't know about God," mused Eli. "Perhaps Elizabeth sent her a note?"

"No, because then Mary could have told us why. The note would be proof," explained Jamie, beaming. "But if it was just a feeling, nobody would believe her. That's why she didn't say anything!"

Miriam stared at him, speechless with admiration as she worked out that the theory fitted perfectly.

Ha, thought Jamie. Now who didn't notice things?

"Yes – but *God...* " said Eli, clearly struggling with the idea of the Almighty being in touch with his youngest daughter.

"Why not?" said Miriam. "Very odd things are happening. I think Jamie is right."

Could Jamie believe his ears? He wondered how long it would take him to learn to write properly, so he could teach her, so she could write 'I think Jamie is right' across a huge piece of parchment that he could stick on his wall. But, more importantly, his beloved Mary had done something noble and kind, just as Jamie had always believed, so everyone would have to think well of her again.

They arrived at Elizabeth and Zechariah's house and fell out of the cart on top of each other, leaving the horse to wander off round the side and park itself. Their urgent hammering prompted a quick reply, as Reuben, the rabbi they'd met at the Temple, flung the door open.

"Well, isn't this a turn-up?" he exclaimed, without bothering with the customary greetings of peace being upon whoever. "Come in, come in!"

He rattled through the social niceties, pointing here and there like a demented airline attendant's pre-flight safety routine: "Cloaks there; drinks there; basin for your feet; basin for your hands; and *there's* the baby!"

And there he was, indeed – a tiny miracle in human form, snoozing on his mother's knee.

"Welcome!" said Elizabeth, the calmest person there. She beamed up at them, but Zechariah, seated next to her with his arms around them both, couldn't take his eyes from his little son, less than three days old. Jamie stood with the others and just stared. How was this possible? Thoughts that the baby might be anyone else's couldn't even creep into their heads. This was no adoption. Elizabeth still had the tell-tale belly bump Jamie had noticed after young women had babies. The new addition to the family may have left the snug hiding place that had kept it safe as it grew, but the mummy's tummy would always take a while to shrink back to how it was before!

The newcomers gazed speechless for some time, and the celebrating neighbours who were already there joined them to gaze again, as if the wonder was so much it needed to be re-done at regular intervals. Reuben the friendly rabbi shook his head, grinning from ear to ear.

"Isn't this a turn-up?" he murmured to himself.

"*How?*" Dinah asked, finally managing to speak.

"The usual way," smiled Elizabeth.

"We are so happy for you!" gushed Eli, then paused, worried in case Zechariah couldn't hear. "HAPPY!" he bellowed, and pulled a grotesque grin. "About the BABY!!!!" he added, rocking an imaginary baby so manically it would have made a real infant puke.

"Honestly!" muttered Miriam to no one in particular. "He's dumb, not stupid."

"CONGRATULATIONS!!" Eli tried again, doing a

happy dance. He translated it into Hebrew with added jazz hands, in case that helped: "MAZAL TOV!!!!"

Zechariah nodded, smiling, to reassure Eli that although he couldn't speak, there was nothing wrong with his ears. Or brain.

Elizabeth saw that the baby was stirring – not surprising, given the racket – and propped him up, moving the wrapping cloths away from his face. "Look, chicken. Here are some of your cousins and friends come to see you."

The baby wrinkled his nose and yawned, his eyes kind of pointing in Jamie's direction and kind of not.

Jamie wasn't sure if such a young babe could focus, or if everyone might just be blurry lumps to him, but he smiled and went closer anyway. "Hello," he said, putting his finger into the fierce grip of the tiny fist, and hoping this smallest and newest of Mary's relatives might see him and know he wanted to be friends.

Mary!

Jamie suddenly remembered the thing that had filled his mind, before this wonder had driven it to the back. He looked at his father and saw that Joseph's eyes were roaming around, hoping Mary would come to greet them from a side room. Elizabeth noticed too, and her face clouded with a hint of concern. It was too small a flicker for anyone to see unless they were looking, but she realised that Jamie had picked up on it and was staring at her, worried. Elizabeth's smile came back, warm and reassuring, as she offered the baby to Jamie.

"Would you like to hold him?"

Jamie was thrilled, sitting next to her so that there would be no danger of dropping him, and Elizabeth slid the long-awaited child onto his lap. "Good practice," she murmured to Zechariah, who laughed a silent laugh.

Jamie had never known anything like it, to have such a tiny being lie completely trusting in his arms. Miriam sat next to him, equally fascinated, and they took turns to cuddle this living bundle of love.

When the community staring had reached a natural lull, Eli cleared his throat, preparing to speak with his least concerned and really-not-worried-at-all voice.

"And, er – Mary? Where is she hiding away?"

He gave a natural, easy smile with his mouth, and a piercing gaze at Elizabeth with his eyes. Joseph's eyes were the same, though he didn't bother with the smile.

"Mary! Sweet girl. Yes, she was staying here," said Rabbi Reuben. "Is she connected to you?"

"She's my daughter," said Eli, not taking his eyes from Elizabeth.

"So kind of her to travel to support Elizabeth through this time," continued Reuben, not picking up on what was really happening.

"Yes," said Eli. "She's very kind."

Elizabeth squeezed Jamie's hand, putting every ounce of reassurance she could into her reply.

"She set off home for Nazareth after this little one was born. You'll see her there when you get back."

Jamie saw the look on his father's face; Joseph had got past the point of believing he'd ever see Mary again.

"You'll be able to talk to her," continued Elizabeth. "I mean, really talk."

"Of course!" exclaimed Eli cheerily, snapping into what must have been Plan R by now in all his excuses for his daughter's odd behaviour. "I should have known. My youngest is ill," he said to all the neighbours. "My poor wife has been run ragged looking after him! How like Mary to go straight home to help, as soon as Elizabeth could spare her."

"You must stay with us for the rest of the feast, Eli," said Elizabeth. "You're family. We'll have the baby's naming ceremony at the end of the festival, and you can go back after that."

"Thank you," said Eli. "Why not? We can catch up

with Mary soon enough."

There was an awkward silence – awkward enough for those not close to the story to start to notice, if someone didn't break it soon. Dinah swooped to the baby, scooping him up.

"May I? Oh, what an absolute darling!"

She took him over to the open shutters as if to look at him properly, cooing over him, and all the neighbours and Eli's family followed, in raptures again.

"You too, Joseph," said Elizabeth quietly, now they were far enough away. "Stay with us. Mary came here to rest and prepare. Let us offer you the same shelter."

Jamie and Miriam watched Joseph, wondering if he would accept. The offer of hospitality, but also the implied hope.

Joseph shrugged, staring at the floor. "Prepare for what?"

Zechariah had tears in his eyes – unable to say anything, and therefore unable to give any comfort. Elizabeth's expression showed as much pain for Joseph, and almost as much difficulty in finding the words.

"What's coming. God's plan for you. Both of you, Joseph – together." Joseph shook his head, but Elizabeth persisted. "She needs you."

"Mary loves you," ventured Jamie, unusually timid, and Miriam nodded eagerly. Joseph didn't even try to respond anymore.

"It's true," said Elizabeth. "Mary loves you, and she loves God. So much."

Joseph wandered out to the elderly couple's patch of land – strolling; standing; staring. Breathing in the peace of the place. He spent a lot of time like that over the next few days, after Miriam and her parents went home – and it did seem to do him some good.

Chapter Twelve
INSERT NAME HERE

Jamie passed the week enjoyably, helping Elizabeth, learning to look after the baby and *trying* to solve the mystery of Mary. Elizabeth was cautious of saying much, but he did get a bit further with his investigations.

"She went before you all got here because she needs to spend time with her mother. And she needs to do that before she sees the rest of you," said Elizabeth as she showed him how to roll out pastry to make sweet treats for the naming ceremony. "Quality time, while just the two of them are at home."

"And Clop," said Jamie, struggling to get pastry out of his hair, but coating it instead with layer upon layer.

"I don't think he'd be much help – but hopefully he won't get in the way. They need to talk, that's all. Here, use a cloth, sweetheart."

Jamie looked at her as he de-glooped himself, not intending to leave the subject till she said more.

"It's not my story to tell," was all he got, so he had to be content with that.

On the eighth day of the festival the neighbours re-grouped in all their finery for the baby's naming ceremony. Joseph had returned to Jerusalem for the last day of observances – but he didn't mind Jamie staying, so Jamie felt very mature to be there alone.

Reuben the friendly rabbi performed the ancient ceremony and everyone stood around the new family to show their support. They got to the moment where the baby would stop being just 'the baby' and take on that word whose meaning would define him and be spoken like a prophecy over his life – his name.

Reuben looked at the proud father, gazing in wonder as always at his little child. He realised there was no point asking him, so he turned to Elizabeth.

"Zechariah, yes?"

The well-wishers sighed their collective approval. That was a noble tradition, to name a son after his father, especially as the father was such a godly man!

"Lovely," said Eli. "Go ahead, please."

"No," said Elizabeth. "His name is John."

This time the neighbours' communal breathing was a slight intake of surprise, muffled by politeness.

"Oh dear," said Eli; "we should have had a little chat before we started. I didn't think there'd be a problem."

"There isn't," said Elizabeth.

No breathing at all, as everyone's eyes flicked over to Eli. Jamie was perfectly placed halfway between them, his head turning repeatedly from one to the other like a spectator in a tennis match. Reuben was also looking keenly between the two − his raised arm of blessing starting to ache, poised over the baby's head, as he cradled him with his other arm.

"But just think, Elizabeth," said Eli, forcing his voice to be very patient as he explained what should *surely* have been obvious; "there's no one in your family with that name on either side, is there? It's a little bit random really, isn't it? So we wouldn't want to upset Zechariah, would we, by giving Baby a name he might not approve of, when he can't do anything to stop it?"

"Zechariah knows his name is John," said Elizabeth with calm clarity.

The neighbours' unison breath commentary on this was a soft, low whistle that seemed to go on forever.

"I see," said Eli to himself, clearly feeling a duty to protect Zechariah's rights and assumed wishes. He prodded Zechariah to get his attention away from baby Zechariah / John / Insert Name Here.

"THE BABY," he bellowed, pointing at the infant and doing his manic rock-a-bye movement again. "WHAT'S HIS NAME?" He gave a huge shrug, his

85

facial expression a wild, exaggerated question.

Zechariah pointed to a slab of wood with a coating of moist clay and a sharp little stick, beckoning for it to be brought.

"Oh, he understood," murmured Eli in surprise at the success of his mime, and rather wishing he'd noticed the writing tablet before he launched out in silly gestures.

"He can hear fine," said Elizabeth, as tactfully as she could.

Everyone except Elizabeth leaned towards Zechariah as he sat to write, like a posse of those dolls that wobble but they don't fall down – looming over him and cutting out the light. He handed the tablet to Reuben, who looked at it, building the suspense, then solemnly read out the winner.

"'His name is John.'"

The synchronised breathers performed a gentle gasp. This, however, switched to a choked splutter as Zechariah leaped to his feet, declaiming loudly in a powerful, steady voice. *Exactly* the voice they had expected outside the Temple, over nine months before.

"Blessed be the Lord God of Israel! – because he has come to visit his people. He has raised up a Saviour for us from David's house so we can be set free from our enemy, just like the prophets said long ago!"

Everyone looked at each other. The old man was talking as if it had already happened. Jamie could hardly stop himself jumping up and down. Messiah? Had he arrived? Would Jamie be able to tell him they were kind-of related, so Jamie was practically a prince?

"He's remembered his promises to us!" shouted Zechariah, as if he'd been desperate to say all this since he had been struck dumb, and it had to come out as fully as possible. "All the mercy he swore to Abraham to give us. It's time. It's now! To grab us back from those who hate us, so we can serve him without fear. We'll be able to be holy and pure in his eyes all our lives long!"

What was this? A quote from some scripture none of them could remember?

Zechariah swung round to speak directly to the child they now knew to be called John, as if this smidgen of life could somehow understand him.

"And you, my little son – you will be called the prophet of the Most High God. You will go before the Lord to prepare his way."

The assembled relatives and neighbours just stared. The prophet? *The* prophet? The one the Holy Writings said was going to shout in the wilderness, telling everyone to get ready for the Anointed Saviour? A sense of awe fell on them in spite of their confusion. Jamie sneaked a look at Elizabeth: she alone did not look the least bit surprised by any of this.

Baby John's eyes shot open, his face lit with the same fire as his father's, his miniature hand stretching as if to grab every word spoken over him. Reuben looked down at him as if he couldn't believe what he was carrying. But Zechariah hadn't finished.

"You will help people understand about salvation and how sins can be forgiven. You will tell them that God's tender mercy means the rising sun will come to us from heaven, to give light to everyone living in the deathly shadows, guiding our feet to the path of peace."

He stopped as suddenly as he'd begun and squeezed his wife's hand as they both gazed at their son.

"Well... Isn't this something?" said Reuben weakly.

It certainly was. Prayers over a new baby were always heartfelt and lovely, and people would say afterwards what a beautiful ceremony it had been – but there was never anything even remotely suggesting the child might have been predicted hundreds of years before to play a crucial role in ushering in the Saviour of the world. Reuben managed to collect himself enough to name the baby and pass him back to his parents, then silence reigned again. People seemed afraid – yet not in a bad way. It looked to Jamie as if they were taking God more seriously; as if they were going to be changed from this point on. As if they would spend the next twenty or thirty years waiting and watching – wondering what John would become.

They continued to stand around gazing in silence, and two or three knelt to pray. When they eventually dispersed to the delicacies laid out for them, their conversation was subdued, about the things of God and what these events might mean.

"Do you think Zechariah's... all right?" murmured Eli to Reuben when the others had drifted out of earshot. "Another seizure, maybe?"

"I think... " said Reuben, trying to gather together exactly what he did think. "I think that I have never known an elderly couple like this to have a child. That it has never happened before that we know of, but for one exceptional time: Abraham and Sarah. That if God has chosen to do such an outstanding miracle again, then Zechariah's behaviour is no illness – in the Temple or now. This is God, Eli. This is real."

Eli slinked over to join the others by the food, trying to grasp all that was happening.

"Hello, John," said Jamie, kneeling to hold the baby's hand again.

John pulled Jamie's hand to his mouth and started sucking on it with his bony gums in a funny, tickly way. Reuben watched with fascination, unable to tear himself away. He stroked the tiny forehead in wonder.

"What did happen in the Temple, Zechariah?" he asked. "What did you see?"

"Who, not what," said Zechariah. "I saw an angel."

"I knew it," breathed Reuben.

Jamie's mind reeled and his mouth opened and shut with nothing coming out, as all the questions he wanted to ask stumbled over each other.

"Taller than this ceiling," said Zechariah, spotting Jamie's desperation and knowing his likely interests. "Like a man, but golden. Beautiful face, shining white robes. Long curly hair. No wings."

"Sword?" Jamie managed to croak.

Zechariah hadn't thought of that. "I don't know; I really didn't notice. I don't think so. He was frightening enough without. It was Gabriel," he added to Elizabeth, who nodded as if she knew all about Gabriel.

"The Temple is very dim inside," Zechariah went on. "One is aware that the walls are lined with gold, but there's only the lampstand to see by. I was approaching the small altar where the incense is burned, when the angel appeared right by it! The Temple was so bright I could hardly keep my eyes open – I could see up to the roof, all those storeys above me – and everything was gleaming gold. Not like him, though. Earthly gold doesn't compare to heaven's glory, and this angel had come straight from heaven."

"What did he say?" asked Jamie, as if this was the most incredible bedtime story ever and he just had to hear the next bit.

"He told me not to be afraid," said Zechariah. "Now I come to think of it, that's often the first thing an angel says to a human – for obvious reasons. I wonder if they ever get bored with it?"

Jamie really wasn't interested in angelic job satisfaction right now. "What did he say next?"

"He called me by my name, and he told me my prayers had been heard. Our prayers, for a child."

He squeezed Elizabeth's hand again, both of them welling up.

"How kind God is!" said Elizabeth, wiping her eyes.

"He said that Elizabeth would have a son," Zechariah went on, "and that we should name him John."

"Controversially!" said Reuben, as they all laughed.

"Eli meant well," said Elizabeth. "He always does."

"I don't think he's quite reached the same level, spiritually, as what is happening," Reuben pondered. "There's been a shift, like a new season, and he hasn't yet noticed the signs of what God is doing."

"He'll need to catch up quickly," said Zechariah, glancing at Elizabeth.

"What did the angel say *next*?" asked Jamie, bouncing and squirming and jigging about on his heels as if anticipating the most wonderful birthday present, or the most urgent trip to the toilet.

"He told me our baby would be a joy and delight to us, which he certainly is – and that many others would rejoice at his birth."

"That's us!" said Jamie with approval that the angel had thoughtfully included him. "We're rejoicing!"

"He said our son would be great in God's eyes, and would live in a special, separate way. And that – he would be filled with the Holy Spirit even from birth."

"The Holy Spirit?" asked Reuben in amazement.

"What's that?" frowned Jamie, wondering why he'd never heard of this before. He felt Rabbi Asher had left way too many gaps around miracles and spirity things. Just wait till he knew an angel had told Zechariah that Jamie himself would rejoice at John's birth!

"The Spirit was only given to a few people, a long time ago," explained Reuben. "They received power directly from God's own Spirit. It's very, very rare."

"Not *quite* so rare in our family," said Zechariah, trying not to sound boastful. "All three of us have received the Holy Spirit."

Jamie and Reuben looked at him, dumbfounded.

"Me, just now, as I regained my ability to speak. Elizabeth and the baby together, while he was still in her womb." Zechariah trailed off, not sure how much more they should tell.

"I was filled with the Holy Spirit when Mary arrived

90

to visit and called my name," said Elizabeth, deciding to hint further since Zechariah's prophetic blurt had shown that God was happy for some of the plan to be known. "I suddenly understood the whole picture, even though Zechariah hadn't been able to tell me. And the baby leaped inside me. He'd heard her voice too."

"Mary?" said Reuben, staring at her very intently.

"Yes," said Elizabeth, with that same gentle firmness she'd shown earlier.

Reuben was about to say more but she flicked her eyes over to Jamie. Reuben understood. He started to pace, shaking his head, with so much to take in. "Mary. Yes, of course."

"*I* think Mary came because God told her about Elizabeth's baby," said Jamie.

"That's right, sweetheart," said Elizabeth, cuddling him. "That's exactly why she came."

"I *told* everyone she came to help," Jamie crowed, pleased that his theory was right.

"Yes, yes. Lovely girl," said Reuben, his mind still racing. "Oh my. And so... Did the angel – "

"Gabriel," said Jamie, keen that this angel who had remembered to include Jamie in his message should get his full due.

"Yes, Gabriel. Did he mention the Messiah thing?"

"He said our John was the one who would go ahead of the Lord in the spirit and power of the long-ago prophet Elijah, turning people's hearts back to God."

"Why couldn't you tell us before?" asked Jamie. "Why did you go all funny?"

"Well, I asked how I could be sure," admitted Zechariah, rather ashamed.

"An *angel* standing there?" gaped Jamie. "Taller than this ceiling, all lit up, and you didn't believe it?"

"It does sound silly when you put it like that," sighed Zechariah. "It just seemed impossible – that the two of us could have a baby of our own. I think the angel was a bit annoyed, to be honest. He pulled himself up to his ridiculously impressive height, and there were these indignant sparks flying off him. 'I am *Gabriel!*' he boomed. 'I stand *in the presence of GOD!*' And because of my doubt, he said I wouldn't be able to speak until it happened. So that was me told."

"Always wiser to trust God, where the impossible is concerned," said Elizabeth, amused.

"Just wait till you have to deal with an angel and see how you get on," smiled Zechariah. "But I didn't really care that I was struck dumb, given the joy in store. I was bursting to tell Elizabeth, but it helped me learn to trust, believing that the truth would be revealed at the proper time, just as Gabriel said."

"So we're going to see Messiah!" said Jamie. "I hope I can meet him. I want to tell him that I'm related to King David too."

"Oh, I'm sure you'll get a chance to do that," said Elizabeth, exchanging a look with the others.

"Where is he?" asked Jamie, peering through the door in case the Anointed One suddenly strolled up the street and popped in to meet his prophet. "Is he here?"

"No, he's not here yet, chicken," said Elizabeth. "But he's on his way."

Chapter Thirteen

AN ANGEL'S WORK IS NEVER DONE

Jamie almost forgot the urgency of seeing Mary in the thrill of his return to Jerusalem the next day. Rabbi Reuben was going to the Temple to teach his followers and kindly offered to take Jamie back to Joseph. And Rabbi Reuben had a shining grey *horse!* Jamie had never seen such a sleek, glossy creature close up. To be lifted high onto it, with Reuben sitting behind in his embroidered robes, made him feel he was taking his rightful place at last. This must be how it was to be a prince! He couldn't believe how far above the ground he was, looking down on everyone they passed. On the open roads it felt like flying as they galloped along – nothing like lumbering in a cart. Reuben held on to him tightly, of course, and was fully in control of the horse, but Jamie felt as if *he* was the one making it speed along as the city came swiftly closer.

They changed to a trot to skirt around the walls to the north, and slid quickly through the crowds of travellers trudging along now the festival was over. Jamie was disappointed to meet up with Joseph at a crossroads, as arranged, to go the rest of the way on his own little legs.

"Shalom, Joseph. God's favour is upon you," said Reuben as if trying to shine God's peace into him, but Joseph didn't notice the difference in greeting.

They thanked Reuben and Jamie waved him off, admiring the handsome charger and making a mental note of the colour and build so that he could get a horse just the same for when he rode into battle in the army of the warrior king who was on his way.

Joseph set off immediately, and there was not much chatter as they walked. It was a kind of race to get back to Mary. Jamie did try to tell him about the amazing things that had been spoken over baby John, but Joseph was used to Jamie prattling on about the Messiah and how he wanted to introduce himself, so he blanked it out. Reuben had warned Jamie that people might find it hard to accept unless God gave them a sneaky peek of it for themselves. Jamie comforted himself that he'd tell Mary when they got back to Nazareth. He was sure she would believe him.

So Joseph was completely unprepared by talk of prophets, messiahs or preparing the way, when he and Jamie knocked at Eli's door late one spring afternoon. They hadn't scrubbed themselves to lobster-like cleanliness; they hadn't even brushed their hair or dropped off the bundles of luggage. Mary would be there, and she wouldn't run away this time. That was all they cared about.

Eli opened the door with reluctance, glancing up and down the street to check no one was watching.

"Joseph. Yes, of course. You'd better come in."

Why was there a look of dread on his face? Jamie had expected this reunion to be happy. He followed his dad in, and – there she was! Mary, lurking in the shadows with her mother, both looking serious. Her eyes and Joseph's met, with so much to say between them that the words stuck.

"Yes. Yes,… we need to… talk… " said Eli, finding it very difficult to do exactly that.

Mary left her mother's side and walked alone to the middle of the room. Jamie stared. She was wearing a light, summery dress that fell in soft folds, and – did her tummy used to look like that? She had always been so slim. It looked more like a small baby bump than too many pastries – but – Joseph hadn't told Jamie he would be getting a new brother or sister so soon. Weren't they supposed to have the wedding first? Jamie looked to his father and saw only shock and uncertainty. Mary placed her hand on her stomach, making the slight bulge clearer, getting rid of any doubt. The shock magnified and mingled with utter grief on Joseph's face.

Mary took a breath, about to speak, but Eli bundled her into a back room with her mother. "I'll deal with it." He shut the door on them and came back to Joseph.

"I see," he said, unable to look Joseph in the eye. "I hoped it might be... That you might know about it."

"I know nothing," said Joseph.

"Yes, I understand," said Eli.

There was a silence when neither Eli nor Joseph could speak, each for their own very different reasons.

"You don't need to worry," said Joseph eventually. "I won't make a big thing of it. I'll put a divorce in place, quietly, with no fuss. As soon as possible. Then they can marry, maybe go somewhere no one knows them. A new start. I truly hope they'll be very happy."

He nearly broke down, and Jamie looked at him in dismay. What was happening?

"You're a good man, Joseph," said Eli, weeping himself. "I am so sorry. I wish I knew what to say to you. I honestly thought she loved you."

"She does!" exploded Jamie. "Mary loves you so much!"

Joseph ignored him, speaking only to Eli. "Start the arrangements as soon as you can. Has she told you whose it is?"

"I can't get a sensible answer out of her," sighed Eli. "Maybe she'll say once she knows you'll give her a divorce. She was probably too afraid."

Joseph nodded, drawing up all his strength as he went to the door. "Tell her I'm not angry. Tell her I understand. I wish her nothing but well."

As Jamie scurried up the street after his father, he heard a noise and turned to see Mary sneaking out of a side door. Joseph hesitated, choked up.

"God bless you, Mary. Be happy," he managed, then turned and walked out of her life.

Jamie ran to her and gave her all the hugs he'd been storing up the last few months.

"What's happening? Why is everybody sad? Why did you run away? Why did your dad put you in that other room? Why won't my dad speak to you? Are you having a baby? Aren't you getting married anymore?"

"I don't know," said Mary, trying to keep track of the questions. "I mean, I know I'm having a baby; I'm not sure about the rest. I need to speak to Joseph."

"Why is he upset? Is it the baby?" asked Jamie. "He said it would be nice for me to have brothers and sisters. And I'm very good at looking after babies now."

"It *would* be nice," said Mary. "We'd be so happy together. Your father is upset because he knows the baby isn't his, so he thinks it must be someone else's. But it isn't, Jamie. It doesn't have a daddy. At least – not a person; not in that way. It's God's baby."

Jamie looked at her with wide, wondering eyes as the wheels in his brain whirred round and round, computing everything he knew, everything he'd learned, everything he'd heard or half-guessed – clicking and clunking at last to one inevitable conclusion, which you, I'm certain, had worked out all along. In fairness to Jamie, he hadn't even quite turned seven, and of course he'd never heard this story before.

He stretched out his hand to her stomach, and that slight evidence of a baby even now taking shape inside her, hardly daring to touch.

"The virgin will have a baby!" he whispered in awe.

"That's it, Jamie! That's exactly it," said Mary, with relief at not having to explain. "There was an angel – "

"Gabriel?" asked Jamie.

"Yes," said Mary, a little surprised. Jamie could tell she was impressed he was on first name terms with angelic beings. "He appeared from nowhere."

"Did he tell you not to be afraid? They usually do," said Jamie knowledgeably.

"That's *exactly* what he said," smiled Mary. "And he called me highly favoured. Me! I couldn't imagine what he meant."

"You're *bigly* favoured, if you're going to have God's baby," said Jamie.

"I know," said Mary. "Elizabeth called me blessed among women – because I was chosen, and because I believed that what God said would happen. I suppose other people will say I'm blessed too, for all the generations to come! The angel told me I'm going to have a son who'll be great and be called the Son of God, and he'll sit on King David's throne and reign forever. I was – well, I was amazed! I asked how it was possible, but Gabriel said it would be a total miracle. Just the power of the Holy Spirit – nothing else."

"You were lucky not to be struck dumb till the baby's born," said Jamie. "Zechariah was, when *he* asked how it was possible."

"Is that what happened?" said Mary. "Elizabeth and I wondered if it might be something like that."

"I suppose there's asking, and there's *asking*," Jamie went on, nodding wisely. "Like, whether you're really doubting or just surprised. Or maybe Gabriel has got used to people asking how. Or maybe he just likes you more. What did you say?"

"I said I wanted God's will for my life, whatever it is. I never expected it to be this, but I've loved God as long as I can remember and I just want to serve him."

"And Gabriel told you about Elizabeth, and that's why you went," said Jamie, with the satisfaction that comes from knowing you were a hundred percent right.

"I knew that if they'd had their own miracle, Zechariah and Elizabeth would be the most likely to believe mine," nodded Mary. "God is turning everything upside down, Jamie. He's filling hungry

97

people with good things, but he's scattering the proud and tipping powerful rulers off their thrones. My spirit keeps dancing around with joy inside me. I just can't help praising God with everything I am! His mercy is flowing out to reach every single person who cares about him, just like he promised all the way back to Abraham and our ancestors. And he's decided to do it through me! Ordinary *me!*"

"I'll tell my dad, and then he'll marry you, and the baby will have a human dad!" exclaimed Jamie, hurtling them all towards their happy ending in his mind. "Do you want the baby to have a human dad?" he added, realising it might be polite to check.

"Very much, as long as it's Joseph," said Mary. "And I think that's what God wants too. But *Joseph* needs to want it, and that's something he can only work out himself, with God."

Jamie sighed at yet more of this people-working-it-out-with-God. It was overrated, in his opinion, as God didn't seem to be in anywhere near enough of a hurry.

"All right, as long as he's quick," Jamie said. "But if he isn't, I'll tell him. So you'd best get your dress ready for the wedding!"

Mary smiled. "I think it'll still just about fit."

Jamie fully intended to give God ten minutes or so to do the necessary, then if Joseph was no nearer enlightenment, Jamie would wade in and sort it himself. But the long journey caught up on him, despite having just heard the best news ever given to mankind.

He fell asleep without even knowing, and had only a dim awareness of his father carrying him to bed and tucking him in. Joseph's subdued weeping long into the night barely disturbed him at all. But it was a very different matter in the early hours of the morning.

Chapter Fourteen

THE GREATEST STORY NEVER TOLD

Near dawn, Jamie was jolted awake by a yell from his father on the other side of the room where they slept.

"Who are you?" shouted Joseph, terrified, flinging his arm protectively in front of his face.

"Probably an angel. Gabriel, I expect," said Jamie, looking around hopefully, then realising his dad was still asleep.

"Do not be afraid... " Joseph muttered, calming.

"Yup, that's an angel," commented Jamie, watching with interest to see if he could catch anything else.

"Mary! My wife... " was next. Promising. Then there was some incoherent mumbling, and something about "save us from our sins" – which was nice, but not as important to Jamie as the Mary-my-wife bit – and then Joseph too jolted awake.

Jamie pretended to be asleep, since God was clearly on the case at last and no longer needed Jamie's help. Joseph gave himself an epic bath, then woke Jamie, insisting he do the same. As Jamie towelled his hair dry, he saw that Joseph had got out their wedding clothes – stuffed to the back of a cupboard for so long, but smelling fresh and not too creased.

Joseph paused at the importance and difficulty of what he was about to explain. "Jamie, this is going to be hard for you to understand."

"Not really," said Jamie. "An angel came to you in a dream and told you not to worry about marrying Mary, because it's God's baby, like Isaiah said."

"Yes," said Joseph, astounded, because he couldn't really say anything else.

"Was the angel called Gabriel?" asked Jamie as he wrestled the wedding tunic over his head.

"He didn't say. How did you... "

"Zechariah pretty much told us. At least, he said baby John was going to prepare the way for Messiah, so, y'know – " Jamie shrugged with an air of what he hoped was casual superiority. "I did try to tell you."

When they knocked at Eli's door, it was with very different emotions from the previous day. Eli was staggered to see them in their finery – but not as staggered as when Mary appeared in her own beautiful dress, surrounded by her mother and sisters.

"The wedding's on again I see," he said with an edge of anger. "I'm relieved, of course, but you might have been honest with me, Joseph."

"I was honest, and so was Mary. Everything she told you is true," said Joseph, smiling at his bride.

"*And* what Zechariah said," added Jamie, keen to play a part in this important moment.

"True?" stammered Eli. "But – how? Our Mary? We're just an ordinary family – it's not possible!"

"Why not?" said Joseph. "None of us was ever really going to be worthy, were we? It had to happen some day, and it had to be *somebody's* Mary, or Abi, or Ruth."

"I know... but... *ours?*"

And all the hurt and misunderstandings of the last few months melted away in laughter.

They quickly made the arrangements, though it was far smaller than the betrothal. What should have been the start of greater respect, position and belonging in the town felt more like the ending of it.

Mary's parents looked on their daughter with pride as they welcomed the guests, but the general feeling was clearly that they should be ashamed of her. Many in Nazareth thought badly of those who didn't do things God's way, and Jamie could tell what people were thinking about the two he loved most in all the world. Rabbi Asher had a nasty smirk on his face, and some of

Mary's brothers glared at Joseph with open hostility. Even Clop was doubtful as Joseph gave him a carved wooden sword to mark the occasion. Tolomai thumped him sharpish to remind him of his manners and normal service was resumed with a cheeky grin of thanks, but it didn't look good for how the other boys might react.

Tolomai's dad was dependable as ever, faithfully refusing to think bad of anyone; that was why they were among the few outside the family who had been invited. He grasped Joseph's hand in congratulation.

"How we got to this point doesn't matter now. All blessings on you, Joseph!"

Joseph took a risk, returning his hearty handshake and lowering his voice. "None of this is how it seems."

Jamie saw the family staring at Joseph as he went to prepare himself for the vows, wondering what he could mean. Jamie caught up with his father, worried that the joyful celebration was being put off too long.

"When are we going to tell everyone the baby is God's?" he whispered.

"We're not," replied Joseph. "They won't believe it just because we tell them to."

"But people think you did something bad!" said Jamie in alarm. "They think you didn't stand by Mary, and you put her through shame."

"They'll think those things of Mary anyway," said Joseph gently. "Her disgrace will be far worse if they know the baby isn't mine. Best if I share it with her."

The angry brothers and the rabbi's sneer far outweighed the calm, steady faces as they began. Jamie said his Hebrew blessing, then had to watch his darling ones stand in silent dignity as they were married in a hurry with scandal hanging over them, allowing people who thought themselves better to heap insults with their looks and think all sorts of evil about them falsely, because of the holy stranger who was on his way.

Then Jamie and Joseph brought Mary back to the lovely home they had prepared for her – tired and happy, a family at last – and what other people thought didn't matter. They felt a little shy, yet a little as if it had always been this way. And it always *would* be this way from now on, for as long as they both lived – Joseph and Mary – Mary and Joseph – their names linked forever, just as we knew they should be.

They let Jamie stay up later than usual as it was such a special day. Mary watched Joseph tuck him in and kiss him good night, then she came to lie on the other side. That was a very good idea. Jamie did get a bit chilly sometimes when he woke up in the night, so he thought it was considerate of Mary to put him between them, where he'd be shielded from drafts. It appeared that Joseph thought it a good idea too, as he also lay down. Jamie snuggled under his blanket, and Joseph and Mary exchanged another of their smiles that went way over his head.

It was only as Jamie dropped off to sleep that something hit him. No matter what the boys at school might think, and no matter how big a miracle it all was – by far the most important thing was that he, Jamie, was going to be the Messiah's actual *brother!*

Life together was as good as they'd hoped, though there are always adjustments to be made, plus the added complication of a baby on the way. Pregnant women often get cravings for something random. Mary's wasn't food-related; she decided she really *really* wanted to go to Jerusalem for the Festival of Weeks. This was partly so that the three of them could stay together; Joseph would have to go, as an adult male, and no way did Mary want to be left behind! Also, she knew how upset Miriam's family must have been at her disappearance. They had wanted to welcome her as a bride, and she longed to see that kind and loving family again; some of

102

her own were still making life awkward. And anyway, this would be her last chance to go to a celebration in Jerusalem for some time. The next one would be the Feast of Tabernacles, which was when the baby was due. There'd be no way she could travel then!

Joseph wasn't going to try and persuade her out of it. He just smiled as he smoothed a plank, intent on the door he was making for a customer. Mary was healthy and strong, and still quite a while off her time. If she was sure she could cope with the journey with a babe on board, that was good enough for Joseph. He didn't want them to be apart either!

They sent word on ahead to their hosts that the groom was bringing his bride this time, and set off early, allowing plenty of time to rest and take it slow. There were also dire warnings to Jamie that there'd be no swinging, or joining in the dance routines. Jamie hoped that as he could usually persuade his dad to do whatever he wanted, he would be able to get round this – but it turned out to be one of those rare times when Joseph wouldn't budge. So Jamie sang and danced on his own for most of the way to Jerusalem, consoling himself that once he got the army of little brothers and sisters he keenly expected, he would teach them the entire set and would never have to dance alone again.

Mary felt it was well worth the journey when they got there. They all did. Dinah had surpassed herself with warmth of welcome, abundance of flowers and succulence of pastries, and even Miriam had curled her hair and put on a smile. There was an awkward moment as Mary took off her travelling cloak and they got their first glimpse of the unmistakable baby bump, but they covered their surprise very well. If Dinah had been determined before that no one should pry into Mary's disappearance and the couple's sudden parting, she went into overdrive now not to think it had any connection to this – so there was much congratulating on both the wedding and the baby news, as if they had all lost the ability to count months.

Jamie was frustrated; surely they could tell *this* family about the God stuff? He'd known them all his life! He was certain they could be trusted, and was itching to tell them that he, of all the boys who'd ever lived, had been chosen to be the Anointed One's brother.

At least there was some chance to talk about it when they went to the Temple. There was Elizabeth with baby John, and Zechariah popping over to see them when he could. The older couple were thrilled and awed in equal measure – happy to see Mary and Joseph together at last, and gazing in fascination at the growing bump that showed God keeps his promises and was sending their Deliverer, slowly but very, very surely.

Anna, too, clearly understood the situation. Jamie didn't dare say anything when he took her a little food offering, as Miriam was with him – but it was obvious from every wrinkle on her shining face that she *knew*.

Jamie took the chance to develop his baby skills, since he now knew what an important job he was about to be given. He reluctantly shared holding little John with Miriam – mainly because Mary made him – though he couldn't see why Miriam wanted to. *She* was never going to have the saviour of the nation put into her care, like he was.

While Jamie and Miriam are in one of their lengthy face-offs over who holds the baby, it gives me time to tell you a bit more about this John. You may already have heard about him: John the Baptist? That's how he became known when he grew up, because that was what he did. He baptised people in the River Jordan – and shouted at the proud ones quite a bit, too – as part of his

104

mission to prepare people for the coming Messiah. But nobody called him John the Baptist yet. They didn't call him John the Anything, because he hadn't really done much – and no loving parents ever called their precious infant John the Pooper, or John the Projectile Vomiter (well, some might, but that would be a different story). So for now we will just call him John – but every time I mention him, you'll know who I mean.

It was nice to be in a large city where not many people knew them. They could walk around as a family without all the stares and whispers. Maybe that was another reason Mary had wanted to come, Jamie wondered – and if so, he agreed with her. It was lovely pretending they were normal. Very few families really are 'normal' – and fewer people – to the extent that it's not even clear if such a dull thing exists. But if you're often the centre of attention, it's certainly relaxing at times not to be noticed.

They mingled with the crowds like undercover superheroes. Jamie took delight in wondering how people would react if they knew. He was pretty sure they would want to tell their grandchildren that one day, long ago, they had passed the Messiah's brother in the street, or let him hold their monkey. But he was starting to see that Mary's way was best. She seemed to store these amazing things up in her heart, as deeply as she carried the baby. Mary did it for the purest of reasons, to treasure what God had done for her – but for Jamie, holding the secret close gave him a warm, superior feeling to all the people around him who didn't know.

Chapter Fifteen

ELEVENTY MILLION AND ONE;
ELEVENTY MILLION AND TWO...

The wonderful break from suspicion and gossip had to end, but they felt refreshed as they got home to Nazareth. Mary especially had enjoyed her last trip for some time to come, but now there was work to be done. It was an exciting time, heady with anticipation, as there were only a few short months until the baby arrived; they needed to get everything ready. They had been entrusted with the most important baby ever, so he must have the best!

Mary worked hard making all his shawls, blankets and little clothes – the wools and linens spun the finest she was able, so that they almost felt like silk. (Mary and Elizabeth were way ahead of their time, of course, in knowing in advance that they were having boys. But they didn't try to colour-code babies in those days, so I doubt they made *everything* blue!)

Joseph crafted a crib beyond what Jamie had ever seen, with swirls of flowers, fruit, leaves and vines all over it. Jamie carefully smoothed beeswax into every detail, polishing till it gleamed. The baby would know he was born to be a king, just from the magnificence of his bed.

In the evenings there was a chance to rest and talk. As Mary got bigger and bigger, and less able to move, Jamie would often sit next to her, cradling her tummy in the hope of feeling the God-child kick. He whispered to his little stepbrother, his mouth pressed close to the folds of Mary's dress.

"I'm going to look after you and help you. And when you fight Herod and the Romans, I'll fight next to you and we'll throw them out together. And you can give me a crown if you want. It doesn't have to be as big as yours, but just so's people can see I'm a prince. I'm your brother, and no one will ever hurt you because I'll protect you."

Everything was going very smoothly as the time drew near. Everything except the Romans – or was it God? Either way, some greater power was adamant that things would not go the way the young couple had planned, and drove them so far from their intended path, the beautiful crib would be covered in cobwebs before a baby would ever use it. The Roman emperor Augustus – or was it God? – decided that everyone should be forced to go back to their town of origin, throughout his whole vast empire, because he wanted to count them.

This might sound like an extreme example of tidying your sock drawer – and it must be admitted that the Romans were rather too fixated with neatness – but Augustus's reasons for knowing exactly who was living in his empire were so that he knew exactly who to keep an eye on, exactly who he could call up into his army and exactly who to tax.

God's reasons, of course, were very different. But when Caesar Augustus decided something, the entire known world had to jump to it – so Jamie and the other boys were startled when a lesson with Rabbi Asher came to an abrupt end, as fathers started turning up early to grab their sons.

"There's a census!" explained Eli breathlessly to the bemused rabbi. "Everyone to their home town, as soon as possible, to swear allegiance to the emperor."

"But there's a feast coming up!" frowned Asher, angry at the lack of respect for their beliefs.

"Tell that to the Romans," agreed Eli. "I mean, don't, obviously. They'd cart you off to prison. Come *on*, Clop. Get your shoes on."

"My strap's got tangled," said Clop, fiddling with it.

"Carry it!" ordered Eli, marching him out hopping –

one sandal in hand, the other on foot but undone, sprawling its straps to trip him. "You too, Jamie," Eli yelled over his shoulder. "Your dad's expecting you at home."

All was confusion as Jamie got back, with Joseph and Mary falling over each other and changing their minds every few minutes over what they should take, who should go, and how long they would be away. Joseph desperately didn't want to leave Mary so close to the baby's arrival, yet clearly there was no way she should be travelling at such a time. The best plan they could come up with was that Jamie should stay at home with Mary, so that Joseph could travel faster alone. Hopefully the Romans would understand; maybe the soldiers here would give him papers explaining why he hadn't taken his family. The village his father had come from was only about a day's walk from Nazareth if he really hurried, so if the Romans were as efficient as they usually were, he could be registered and back before Mary needed his support. She would be safe here, especially if her mother or one of her sisters could perhaps stay back to help her. Jamie heartily approved of the plan since it left him in charge as the man of the house – in his own eyes, at least.

Until a Roman soldier called at the door to check on their preparations.

"Which tribe?" he snapped, without bothering with a greeting. The Romans never wished peace on anybody, but they did at least usually bark something about health in Latin.

"Oh – Judah," said Joseph, surprised at the question.

"Judah, Judah... " muttered the soldier, trawling through his scroll. "Which family?"

Joseph was puzzled. Did he really want the whole 'Joseph, son of Jacob, son of Matthan, son of Eleazar, son of Eliud' thing? He wasn't sure how far back he could go without having to look it up.

"Which ancestral line?" sighed the soldier, fed up with all the Hebrew names that were hard for him to pronounce, and all too aware of how many more houses he had to go.

"We're descended from King David," said Jamie haughtily, hoping the soldier would realise the implications and know that his days of bossing them about were numbered.

"David, son of Jesse," said the soldier, winding to the right bit of the scroll. "Born in Bethlehem; get to it."

Mary turned pale and had to sit down. Joseph looked at him aghast. Bethlehem in *Judea?* The pitiful little village whose name was hardly worth the ink it took to write it on a map? That was all the way to Jerusalem!

"What?" asked Joseph weakly, hoping there must be some mistake. "My family hasn't lived there for many hundreds of years."

"David's line: Bethlehem, also known as Ep... Eph... rathah," confirmed the soldier, doublechecking the all-important scroll. "That's where you're headed, sharpish. Well, quick as possible," he added less roughly, seeing how close Mary was to her time. Having dropped his bombshell he left them to it, giving an awkward nod to Joseph as if, in a different world, they might have been friends. But they weren't in a different world; they were in this one, and they had to deal with it.

Jamie watched his father, wondering what the new plan would be and whether he would still be left in charge, but something very different was going through Joseph's mind.

"Bethlehem. Of course. I'm so sorry," he said. "I should have thought. I'd totally forgotten."

Mary looked at him, blank, as Joseph wracked his brains to remember.

"It's the prophet Micah. 'But you, Bethlehem Ephrathah, though you're small among the people of

Judah, out of you will come someone whose origins are of old – from ancient times. He will rule Israel for me, and stand in the strength of the Lord to shepherd them like a flock.'"

"David?" asked Jamie. He had been a shepherd boy, before he became king.

"No. Messiah," said Joseph. "That passage was written long after the time of David. There's even something about 'she who is in labour' giving birth in Bethlehem."

He glanced at Mary, whose head was swimming with how many prophets had written about her all those hundreds of years ago, and what she now had to do.

"I'll borrow a donkey for you to ride on," Joseph promised. "No, I'll buy one. I'll find something to sell. But... it looks like it has to be Bethlehem."

They set about the task, splitting up to achieve things more quickly. Mary started packing, steadfastly choosing which very few of the baby's things they'd be able to take. Joseph searched for a spare donkey he could buy – a fruitless task, amidst a whole town of people about to go on unexpected journeys thanks to this all-powerful disruptor. Jamie headed to the baker's.

Other children were on the same errand, hurriedly fetching the bread their mothers had brought in earlier in the day to cook in the large ovens, now urgently needed so they would have something to eat on the journey. Jamie's classmates were swapping news of where they had to go; no one else had a journey like Jamie's ahead of them.

Tolomai paused a moment from trying to work out which loaves were his mother's when he heard what Jamie told them, as if the destination had pinged some buried memory.

"Bethlehem?" repeated Clop in amazement. "Which tribe did your dad tell them?"

"Judah," said Jamie. "I thought you were Judah

too?"

"Yeah, David's gang," said Clop. "But Dad told the soldiers we're Zebulun. Loads of them lived round here in the old days – we're only going up the road. Get your dad to go back and say he forgot!"

"No," said Jamie bravely, trying to make his pronouncement sound as weighty as it honestly was. "It has to be Bethlehem."

Tolomai turned to stare at Jamie with a weird look on his face. "'But you – Bethlehem Whassisname – even though you're so titchy... '"

"That's right," said Jamie, willing him to guess right there in front of everyone. A rumour that started in the bakery was guaranteed to go all round the town before the dough had time to rise, and it would be so cool if everyone knew and came to wave them off. Maybe weeping a little at how badly they'd treated them? Realising how wrong they had been, and how much more worthy Jamie was to be related to the Chosen One. But whatever earth-shaking conclusions Tolomai was jumping to, unlike Jamie, he wisely and infuriatingly knew the importance of guarding his tongue.

Not put off, Jamie remembered the sturdy donkey Tolomai's father owned, and tried another tack to capitalise on this dawning realisation.

"We just need a donkey now," he mused, as if thinking aloud. "For Mary to ride, to keep her and the baby safe."

"I'm on it," said Tolomai. "I mean... not literally." And he scooped up some random loaves and rushed out.

He was true to his word. They were the proud owners of a donkey within no time, and had barely finished getting their things together when the soldiers came around again, ordering everyone to get going.

And that is how it happened that the Romans and

their unhealthy obsession with counting things, and God's mighty plan, fixed from ancient times, collided into one perfect storm so great it was about to split Time itself into 'before' and 'after', and chased our little family and a second-hand donkey on to the long, hard road to Bethlehem.

Chapter Sixteen

THE SURPRISINGLY GOOD SAMARITANS

It was a very different feel from the usual treks south to Judea. No streams of happy pilgrims, all going in the same direction, excited for the feast and trying to avoid Jamie's songs. Everyone was worried, everyone was headed somewhere different, and there were Roman soldiers watching them at every crossroads. They didn't hurry Jamie's group, once they saw Mary's condition, but plenty of other families got shouted at for dawdling. It felt to Jamie as if they had to go much more quickly than was comfortable for Mary, or they would be the next to get a Roman curse or a cut of the whip.

The views were strange, as well; Jamie had never been this way before.

"Shouldn't we have gone left before now?" he asked, wondering if the staring soldiers had confused Joseph. "We'll end up in Samaria soon, if we're not careful."

The people of Samaria were not a friendly bunch in those days – not to Jewish people, anyway, and vice very-much-versa. It was strange, as they were sort of related to each other if you took it way, way back, but sometimes family arguments are the worst. It was well known that Samaritans would not offer hospitality to Jews, *particularly* if they knew they were travelling to a feast in Jerusalem. They thought their ways and places of worshipping God were better, which was why all the Jewish people from Galilee Jamie knew would rather go the long way round and risk the snakes and lions in the wilderness than ask a Samaritan for permission to cross their land.

"We need homes to stay in," said Joseph tersely. "And we need to go the shortest, most direct way. We're going through Samaria."

Mary was startled. "Will they let us? I thought they hated us."

"They'll see how close you are to your time," said Joseph. "They aren't bad, just different. And anyway, they hate Roman rule as much as we do. They'll have been messed about by the census too. We'll say our journey is the Romans' fault."

"It *is* the Romans' fault," muttered Jamie, wondering how soon his little brother would be able to hold a sword.

The plan worked. Each day they went as far as Mary felt able, the donkey plodding patiently down the merchants' trade road south, then they looked for a village to stay in. Ginae, Sychar, Shiloh, Ephraim – it didn't matter where; Joseph would ask around the few people left for a room to stay in, a little food and water, and straw for the donkey. Most families they stayed with were suspicious of them to some extent. The flavours of the food were strange to Jamie, and the names of the children even stranger: Omri, Baasha, Asenath, Photina... But these Samaritans shared what they had, and the next day gave food and water for the onward journey and waved them off, the same as a Jewish family would.

Some of the place names were familiar to Jamie from the rabbi's classes. Wasn't this the way their ancestor Abraham had come, right back when God had told him to leave his land and go on a journey? And where Isaac, Jacob and their families had lived, as they wandered from place to place? The Samaritans certainly seemed to think so. Jamie often heard phrases like 'our father Abraham and our mother Sarah' thrown around by them as confidently as a Judean or Galilean would say it, when the grown-ups talked politics, history and religion as he dropped off to sleep. They really must be related to each other somehow, Jamie supposed – though, from what you know of Jamie, you won't find it hard to believe he was happy to think that *his* was the better and more important branch of the family. God was sending his Messiah to them, not to these Samaritans!

"Are you all right?" Joseph would ask Mary from time to time as they travelled on, and she would nod and smile, not saying much, her jaw clenched shut. Often Joseph would walk alongside her, and she'd lean her elbow on his shoulder and push herself up, so that her weight wasn't always in the same place. Tolomai's dad had included a thickly padded saddle with the donkey, but it wasn't comfortable to be riding every day.

Sometimes Mary would wince, and Joseph always noticed straight away.

"What is it? Is the baby starting?"

"No," Mary would say. "It's just a twinge" or "It's just the donkey jolting about."

There was nothing to mark the border, but it was noticeable when they crossed from Samaria into Judea. Not in the types of house – not in the way the people looked – not even in the landscape – but Jamie could tell from the clothes and the accents that they were back among Jewish people, even though Judea was so very different from Galilee, where he came from.

The more familiar territory was unnervingly strange compared to usual, because of the census. As they got closer to Jerusalem they saw that some people had built shelters for the feast, yet not many seemed to be getting ready to live in them. The Romans had disrupted everyone.

The oddest thing of all was to see that first glimpse of Jerusalem. Jamie had always been so excited for it, yet what was the point of looking, since they weren't going there? No cakes, no catching up with friends, no celebration at the Temple. Bethlehem drove them, along with the little stranger destined to be born there: a Holy One from ancient times, yet coming to live with them as one of their family.

As they came to the crossroads where Rabbi Reuben had dropped him off – one road leading up the last slope to the Damascus Gate, the other skirting around the city walls – Jamie suddenly realised what day it was. Sunset wasn't far off and then it would be the Feast of Tabernacles, the season to be joyful, Jamie's absolute favourite! None of them had meant to attend, even Joseph, what with safe delivery of the Messiah rather trumping any other priority on the list – but now that they were here, by freaky coincidence, at exactly the right time...

Jamie was opening his mouth to say it made sense to stay in Jerusalem tonight, as it would be nearly dark by the time they got to Bethlehem, when Mary gave a sharp gasp, leaning forward and grabbing the saddle.

"What is it?" asked Joseph quickly. "Is the baby starting?"

She didn't answer straight away, holding on tight. Jamie and Joseph stared at her, sensing the difference.

"I'm not sure," she said. "It might be."

"Noooooo!!! What is God doing?" groaned Jamie. "All those thousands of years to prepare, and he leaves it this last minute?"

"It's not God's fault!" said Joseph, desperate for Mary and angry at himself. "He put it all there for us, in the writings. It's me. How could I have been so stupid? I should've remembered and brought us to live here as soon as we married."

Mary unstiffened, straightening up cautiously.

"It's not your fault either," she said, the only one staying calm. "Scholars spend their lives arguing over the scriptures. No one can remember it all."

"Oh well, we tried," sighed Jamie, wondering if

Miriam's family might be home after all, and whether Dinah had been baking today. "God will understand."

He hitched his pack more comfortably onto his shoulders and started up the road to Jerusalem.

Mary shook her head. "It has to be Bethlehem. Come on, God is with us. He'll help us."

Jamie watched in disbelief as she nudged the donkey onto the path around the city, with Joseph drawing up his strength and going with her. Seriously, could they not just pop to Jerusalem? Was that not a more fitting place for the King of kings to be born – a capital city, with all those golden buildings? Did it have to be that stupid little village, the smallest of the small? This was an emergency! The rules had changed. God could not reasonably expect them to stick with something written hundreds of years ago! Who knew if this Micah was a proper prophet anyway? Maybe he had friends in Bethlehem, and was just trying to help them with a bit of publicity. How much more sensible it would be to find shelter in a closer, bigger place where there would be far more choice of where to stay, and get Mary comfortable in plenty of time. Joseph could easily travel from Jerusalem to register for the census, and they could always take the baby to Bethlehem for a visit when he was a few days old, if it really was *that* important to God.

Mary and Joseph pressed on without even looking back to see if Jamie was following, and he was quickly getting left behind, so – for the first time, but by no means the last – Jamie had to abandon any ideas that his way was the best, and run to catch up with God's plan.

Bethlehem was even less interesting than Jamie's very low expectations. He'd glimpsed it from the road when they went to visit baby John, but as they approached it became clear the village was little more than a settlement of a few hundred shepherds and farmers. That was all they ever did here: produce the lambs to be taken to Jerusalem for Passover and the other offerings. Jamie could see a flock of sheep out on a distant hillside right now.

None of the houses was new or even in good repair, and though Jamie had always lived in a poor home himself, he was a snob when it came to other people. He hoped Joseph could find somewhere decent. But as they got into the village itself, a new problem began to dawn on them. You remember all those people, descended from King David? All those people with as much right to think themselves princes and princesses as Jamie? Here they all were, to register with the Romans. All right, *some* may have lived near enough to travel there and back in a day. Some may have journeyed very quickly and been processed ahead of the rush, then gone home. Some may even have been as quick-thinking as Eli, to give a fake tribe close to where they lived – but this family reunion was clearly a great deal bigger than was comfortable, even with many folks staying in the shelters that had been made for the Feast of Tabernacles.

Joseph stopped and stared at the throng of people, dismayed at this last hurdle just when he thought they had reached their goal. He couldn't even see where to begin, but another sudden gasp and clinging to the saddle from Mary pushed him into action.

"'On the mountain of the Lord, it will be provided,'" he muttered to himself, quoting from the Holy Writings and striding towards the buildings.

Chapter Seventeen

MUCH-TOO-LITTLE TOWN OF BETHLEHEM

What *exactly* would be provided on the mountain of the Lord, Jamie wondered? To say 'it' would be provided seemed a bit vague, and this shabby village filled with sweaty travellers was no grand mountain.

Joseph knocked at the first door with commanding urgency. A small girl opened it, with an even smaller girl wailing and clinging to her.

"Who is it?" yelled a woman from further in the house, nearly drowned out by the sounds of more crying children, and hidden from sight by a crowd of travellers, still with their cloaks on, packed too tight to sit, eating their dinner standing up. "Tell them we're full."

"We're full," whispered the girl apologetically, closing the door in Joseph's face.

Joseph knocked at the next door with a tad less authority. It was opened a sliver almost immediately by a weasel-like man who glared at them, glancing furtively up and down the street.

"Password?"

"My wife is about to give birth,..." said Joseph.

"That was *last* year's password," snapped the man. "Ain't you got nothing more current?"

"It is current," said Joseph, wrong-footed. "It's happening now!"

From inside the dim room with its closed shutters, Jamie heard a group in heated debate:

"If we want people to join the revolution, we have to have the right name!"

"All I'm saying is, 'Judean, Samaritan and Galilean' is too long."

"'Judean, Galilean and Samaritan' flows better..."

Were they the resistance movement? Jamie had

heard of such people, but he'd never met any before.

"We want to get rid of the Romans too!" he broke in, hoping it would make them welcome in this strange house. "The baby who'll be born tonight is the Chosen One who's going to do it. We'll join with your group, when you've decided what to call it, and we'll fight together."

"Not without the password, you won't," retorted the man, slamming the door.

Joseph knocked at another door with even less confidence, already hearing the din.

"HANG ON A MINUTE!" bellowed a woman's voice, and then followed a stream of interrupted monologue to the people inside: "Yes, could I just squeeze... I just need to get through... Could you just pop those chickens on the... " (Loud squawking, and a lot of flapping) "So kind. I'LL BE RIGHT WITH YOU!!" she bellowed again. "Sorry, dear, can I... If you'd just lift the ram's horn so I can duck... " (Tuneless toot from a ram's horn) "Smashing, thank you. Yes, do put your cloaks on Grandad, he won't... COMING!!! Can I just get past... No, careful of the slop bu– oh, never mind... Is that your goat? Could you just... " (Outraged bleating) "Perfect... I'm just trying to... Ah, there we are."

The door burst open with a loud blast from the ram's horn and more clucking and bleating, and the woman spilled out of her house on a tide of people and animals.

"Yes, dear. How can I help?" she said brightly to Joseph, with the smile of one so used to giving the appearance of coping she did it even when no one could possibly believe her.

"My wife is having a baby," said Joseph, desperate for someone to listen.

"Goodness, so she is!" said the woman looking at Mary, who was leaning forward again, clutching the donkey's mane and doing strange panting instead of normal breaths.

"Is there an inn in this village?" asked Joseph, hoping against hope. It wouldn't be like a proper hotel, but sometimes people built on extra rooms and opened up their houses to give hospitality, as a way of earning a living. It was clear no ordinary home would have space for them tonight.

"Ah. Thing is, this *is* the inn," said the woman with the same bright smile, her eyes glazing over with the vastness of the problem. "It's the Romans, you see."

"We know," said Joseph, unable to cope with any more opinions about the Romans right now.

Mary gave a groan, trying hard not to make a noise.

"Right then," said the woman, making her mind up, leaning past random guests and trying to reach into her home. "Could I just... Yes, would you mind, dear? If you'd just prop that big slab of cheese up above the... Sorry, Grandad... Thanks... There we are... "

She prised herself back out with difficulty, brandishing a rusty key and lowering her voice.

"You see that animal shelter, just outside the village?" They looked and saw a ramshackle old building, once a watchtower but now mostly crumbled to just one storey, standing by itself. "It's mine," she continued, slipping the key to Joseph. "I've been saving it for me and Grandad, with all this craziness, but – well – your need is greater! There's a few cows and that, but the straw is clean, and it's warm and private."

"Thank you, thank you!" gasped Joseph with heartfelt gratitude, and even Jamie's picky standards had dropped so far, he gave her a big tearful hug.

"I'll bring you some food out when I can," said the kind but flustered innkeeper lady, as a cry of "More wine! More wine!" started up inside, accompanied by enthusiastic ram's horn action.

Mary nodded thanks to her, and they moved off to

their own private residence for the night. As they went along the street – now lit by the full moon, it was so late – Jamie saw the innkeeper trying to herd her guests back inside and close the door.

"If you could just... Yes, that's... Coming, dear, just give me a... Could I just squeeze... If you could let me in... Yes, right away, sir!... If I could just... Let me in, please... Just let me... It's MY HOUSE!!"

The kind innkeeper was right about there being a few animals in her shelter, but also about the clean straw and the warmth. If anything, two cows, a cart horse and five goats made it even snugger, once you got used to the smell, and it was much quieter than the teeming village.

Jamie carefully helped Joseph get Mary down from the donkey, then he plumped up the straw into a kind of beanbag shape that would be more comfortable under her than the hard, earthen floor – and would prop her up from behind, too – and Joseph supported her down on to it. She lay back on the straw and nodded to them that she was all right, doing her funny breathing again.

While Jamie held her hand, Joseph looked around and found a lantern, whipping out the little flint he kept in his belt to light fires and quickly getting the wick burning. That was better. Looking around some more, he found a big, heavy pitcher of water and brought it to Mary, lifting it to her lips so she could drink.

"Isn't that for the animals?" asked Jamie, wrinkling his nose.

"Probably," said Joseph, "but it hasn't gone in their drinking trough yet, and water is water."

He drank some himself, and Jamie had a long slurp too, realising that he was also very thirsty and that water is indeed water.

Jamie thought that now they were safely in the broken-down building, Mary would simply have the baby – but apparently there was more to it than that, with puffing and panting along the way. The animals watched with interest. They had taken the donkey to their hearts right away, but were reserved and politely curious when it came to the humans.

The innkeeper arrived as soon as she could get away, with food and a bucket of steaming hot water, soap and towels.

"There we are. All right? Not long now," she smiled encouragingly to Mary, who nodded back, a little too busy to smile. "I'd stay and help, but... "

"Don't worry, you've done enough," said Joseph. "Go back to your guests. God is with us, we'll be fine."

Now Mary did manage a smile. "Immanuel," she murmured, lying back to rest between puffing bouts.

Jamie escorted the innkeeper to the door, longing to tell her what earth-shattering event was about to take place in her ruin, but she heard more rowdiness from the inn and hurried off. Couldn't they tell *anyone?* Did God intend this whole thing to be top secret until the freedom army marched on Jerusalem, trumpets blazing, behind Jamie and his brother on their white horses?

He was about to close the door when he noticed the moon. It had turned a deep, dusky rose colour such as Jamie had never seen before, though he had heard that this happened from time to time. How beautiful! He went outside to admire it properly and stood there staring at it, until he remembered he should probably go back in and help.

As he was turning away, he caught the briefest flash of light in the clouds some distance away. Was a thunderstorm coming? It didn't feel like it. The weather wasn't hot and unbearably clammy – although – it might have been Jamie's imagination, but he did feel that slight tingle of hairs standing up on the back of his neck that was a sign lightning was in the air.

Jamie waited to see if there would be another flash.

He liked storms, the wilder the better. For a moment he thought he had been mistaken, but then it showed again; just a glimmer, over the Bethlehem hills. And then darkness once more.

Was that it? Disappointing. He should definitely go back in; he didn't want to miss anything.

But *then* – oh, how can I tell you? – how will you ever believe me? – The sky ripped open as if they had been living in a thick sack all this time without knowing, and someone outside the sack had decided to tear a long gap in it to let real light shine in for the very first time. Strange beings poured through – more and more and more of them, circling and swooping and filling the sky over the hills – as if whatever place was on the other side of the rip was emptying to come and be with the people of earth.

Jamie dropped to his knees, terrified, even though he was at a distance. What was happening? What were these vast, fluid creatures, alight with unearthly fire?

A fireball of liquid gold shot down onto the hilltops and a commanding voice drifted faintly across the night air: "Do not be afraid!"

Angels!!! Jamie gasped as if he would never breath again. He had vaguely hoped that God might one day light up a few Gentiles, or that Gabriel might decide he ought to introduce himself to the Messiah's brother, but this was something else. An *army* of angels, there in front of his eyes, more than he could ever count, as they merged into each other and split again in a strange eternal dance while music played, unlike anything Jamie had heard before.

Was Gabriel there among them? Was he perhaps the spokes-angel? Jamie couldn't imagine that Gabriel would have missed it, and yet they were all so glorious it made him dizzy trying to watch them individually to see if any looked more important than the others.

Once all the angels were through to our side, the rip from Eternity into Time closed abruptly and the hills went dark again, leaving only the ethereal light from the angels to ripple over the fields.

"I bring great news, unending joy – to you, and to everybody," went on the voice, which Jamie could only just catch in snippets, carried on the breeze. "Your Saviour is born this very day, in David's town. The Lord. The Anointed One!"

Born? He was born at last? Jamie turned wildly back to the open door, where the feeble light of the lantern spilled into the darkness in answer to the angel glow. The unmistakable first cry of a baby cut with discordant, frail humanity across the heavenly sounds. Jamie wanted to go and look but his legs were too wobbly. He was frozen to the spot, clinging weakly to the ground on all fours.

The other angels scooped down towards the hills into a circle formation around the first one, like a crown of light. There was the singing of a myriad unearthly voices, harmonising and crossing as perfectly as they danced.

"Glory to God in highest heaven and peace to the people of earth. His favour is on you!"

Still the angels circled and weaved, soaring ever higher until eventually Jamie could barely see them and the music faded almost to nothing.

Chapter Eighteen
O, SHEEPISH NIGHT

Jamie gulped a few hoarse breaths. Had anyone else witnessed the angels? Bethlehem seemed to be carrying on as usual – no one else had come out to stare. How could they all miss it?

He managed to crawl and stumble his way back to the old building. He meant to tell them what he'd seen, but when he entered he forgot about the wondrous visions outside, entranced by Mary and Joseph's looks of joy. A new parent's face shines, you know – in a very ordinary, everyday way – with just as much beauty as the glory of heaven.

Joseph was reclining on the straw next to Mary with his arm around her, and they both gazed in adoration at the tiny, wrinkled wonder in her arms. When they saw Jamie, they looked up at him with smiles as bright as any angel beam. Jamie crept forward, not wanting to frighten the baby, unable to believe that their Saviour had been entrusted to them. For a short time, at least, he felt very humble and in need of God's help. He snuggled up with them, marvelling at being able to cuddle and kiss the miracle baby.

Something important suddenly occurred to him. "Did Gabriel tell us what to call him?"

Mary and Joseph exchanged a glance, each wondering if the other knew. They smiled as they realised they both did, and said it together:

"Yehoshua."

Jamie heartily approved. It meant 'the Lord saves' which seemed an excellent name for someone who was going to rescue them from oppression as soon as he could hold a sword. It was the name of the great warrior who had led them into the land God had promised them, and could be pronounced Joshua, like that warrior guy – but Hebrew speakers would tend to say Y'shua and most people would end up calling him something like the Greek version, Jesus.

They remembered the food the kind innkeeper had brought them, and picked at it while Mary gave baby Jesus his first supper.

"We should wrap him up warm and put him where he can sleep," she said when he had finished, not really wanting to tear herself away from her firstborn child. She would have loved to keep him safe there in her arms forever. "Pass me that bundle please, Jamie?"

Jamie opened the bundle and got out one of the very few baby things they had brought – a long, simple cloth, which Mary wrapped round and round as they did in those days, until only his little face was peeping out, like a very cute cocoon. She looked around, at a loss where to put him to keep him safe, and for a moment they all felt a pang of regret as they remembered the beautiful crib back in Nazareth. None of this had turned out as they had hoped – *nothing* that had happened was a part of their plan – yet here they were, and all was well. God was with them in a deeper way than they had ever known, and had provided everything they needed, on his own terms, beyond human understanding. Even a crib, it seemed – bizarrely. Mary's eyes lit up as she spotted a manger, filled with fresh hay for the animals.

"Perfect!" she laughed, laying the baby in it. It did seem a fitting and very quirky detail to round off the whole astonishing night. "Sleep well, my Y'shua" she whispered, kissing his forehead.

The animals seemed happy with the arrangement, watching over the little intruder in their feeding trough with soft, patient eyes. A cow wandered over to give him a snuffly kiss, which made him sneeze. That would be frowned upon nowadays – but then, cows are rarely allowed in modern hospitals, as you may have noticed.

As Time had been successfully split in two and the momentous event foreseen from ancient days was achieved, the four of them drifted happily off to sleep.

They were disturbed, probably not that much later, by rowdy chatter some distance away. Jamie was annoyed; could the people crammed into Bethlehem not settle down and have a little consideration? This had been a very tiring day for Jamie and his family.

"There's a light in the old watchtower!" a child shouted.

Jamie realised that the rough voices were praising God, and it hit him – other people had heard the angel's announcement after all! Maybe this was the first of many who would come; he could show them the baby and tell them the whole story of how he, alone of all boys, had been chosen to be brother of the King. Jamie decided he had better get used to being this famous, with crowds flocking to listen to him at any time of the day or night.

As Mary and Joseph sat up blinking, rubbing sleep from their eyes and making themselves presentable, Jamie dashed eagerly outside to greet their visitors.

It was only a bunch of shepherds, but maybe the angels hadn't been able to find anyone better. These would do to begin with, Jamie supposed, so he flung his arms out wide to say something very profound and memorable.

"Yep, there's the manger, Dad. I can see it through the door!" yelled a boy younger than Jamie, pushing past him without even noticing.

"Is there a baby in it?" asked one of the men, pressing forward eagerly.

"Think so. There's something," said the boy.

The whole rabble of shepherds stampeded towards the wrecked building, jostling Jamie to one side. He was outraged. Didn't they know who he was? They couldn't be very godly, not to realise his importance and treat him with respect.

Bringing up the rear was a surprisingly sturdy little girl, her big eyes peering over the lamb she carried, nearly the same size as her.

"I'm going to show him my lamb," she said solemnly to Jamie as she stomped past.

"It's not *your* lamb," hissed the little boy over his shoulder, reaching the building. He craned in, looking at the feeding trough and bounced on the spot in delight, beckoning the others. "This is it! Come on, he's here. Our Saviour, Christ the Lord!"

Joseph came to the door to greet them as they all rushed in. "Welcome! Peace be with you."

"I'm going to show him my lamb," the solid little girl informed him as she entered.

"Right. Lovely," said Joseph.

Jamie was still staring at them indignantly when he was butted out of the way by the lead sheep of an entire flock, trotting cheerily along the overgrown track to the ruined tower and piling in after their shepherds. There were so many of them, Jamie could barely get close enough himself to see what was going on.

"I'm sorry," he heard the little boy say to Joseph. "We did tell them to stay, but sheep don't understand words. Or anything, really."

Mary smiled at the shepherds, lifting the baby out of the trough so they could see him better, and a hush fell. Every one of those rough-looking field workers dropped to their knees in worship, some of them crying openly. When Jamie got close enough to look in, he saw that Joseph and Mary were gazing just as adoringly at the baby Saviour as the shepherds were. The angels swooped low, paying their own tribute, circling above the building. Even the animals had expressions of peaceful trust as they gazed steadily at the baby. Jamie became uncomfortably aware that his was the only grumpy face around. But surely he couldn't be expected to kneel and worship his own *brother?*

Joseph and Mary had endless patience, letting the shepherds spend as long as they wished praising God for sending his son. Then the reverential silence was broken as the men left, chattering noisily, keen to tell everyone they knew – followed by their sheep, chattering just as noisily in their own woolly way.

"I showed him my lamb," announced the little girl to Jamie as she trooped out, still clutching the long-suffering animal. The little boy followed.

"It's not your lamb! The lambs belong to all of us."

"It is," she replied with dogged determination. "It's my lamb."

"I'm sorry, she can be difficult," said the boy to Jamie. "Hello. I'm Adam, and this is my sister Evie."

Jamie stared at him, not sure whether to believe it. Seriously? Their parents had done that to them? Adam was used to that look when he told people their names.

"Mum and Dad don't have much imagination," he sighed. "I think they just started at the beginning."

Before Jamie could reply with his name, the sky ripped open once more and they were flooded with that realer-than-real light from another place as the angels flew back home.

Evie strode out and tilted her face to the light, bawling at the departing angels and right into heaven itself: "I SHOWED HIM MY LAMB!"

An angel at the rear of the throng turned back and gave her a big grin and a nod before he too dodged through the gap and it zipped up tight, leaving them with the ordinary night sky, lit by the ordinary moon.

"I'm Jamie," said Jamie, once he was sure the celestial firework display had finished.

They peeped back into the tumbledown building,

where Mary and Joseph had nodded off to sleep. Jamie could tell Adam and Evie were longing to spend more time with the baby without their grown-ups, so he beckoned them back in. The three children clambered up onto a hay bale by the manger – not an easy task, since Evie refused to let go of her lamb – and perched in a row, gazing at the baby and talking in whispers.

"His name's Y'shua, or Jesus," said Jamie, realising with a shiver that he might be the first person to introduce the Saviour-king to others by name.

"What a lovely little lamb," said Evie, beaming at him over the woolly back of her own little lamb.

At last Jamie got the chance to tell the story of what had happened, but it wasn't how he had expected. Sitting there, looking at the baby, everything seemed to be about him, not Jamie. It actually felt nicer that way.

Adam and Evie were a good audience, sighing in satisfaction as he got to the end.

"What about you?" asked Jamie. "Did you hear about it from the angel?"

"It was us he come to speak to," nodded Adam. "He landed slap bang in front of us, like a shooting star."

"Or a piece of lightning," said Evie.

"Lightning comes in bolts, not pieces," corrected Adam. Evie's face remained set; she clearly thought her word was better.

"We're shepherds, you see," continued Adam.

"Yes, I thought so," said Jamie, not liking to point out it had been stupid-obvious from their clothes, their smell and the sudden influx of sheep. "I'm a carpenter myself."

"While we was watching our flocks tonight, all sitting round our fire – " said Adam.

"All seated on the ground," interrupted Evie.

"*Obviously* on the ground. We wouldn't have chairs, would we?" said Adam, irritated. " – up on the hills,

131

with Dad and our uncles – "

"What were you doing all the way up there at night?" asked Jamie. It seemed odd behaviour, even for people whose lives revolved around sheep.

"It's the only place there's much grass, this time of year," explained Adam. "They've ate the rest. We have to keep going further out, till the rains come and everywhere goes green again."

"Shouldn't you be in Jerusalem for the Feast of Tabernacles?" asked Jamie.

"'Tis the season to be jolly," commented Evie to herself.

"*Joyful*," said Adam. "Nah, we end up missing quite a few festivals. We can't leave the sheep alone, see. Not that close to the wilderness and all the wild beasts."

"Rrrrrraaaaaaaaaaaagh," said Evie, trying to make her hands like ferocious claws without dropping her lamb. Joseph muttered, stirring in his sleep. Adam shushed her and continued in a whisper.

"Someone's always got to stay out with them to protect them. Especially the lambs."

"And this one's mine," said Evie with a defiant look.

"So there we was," said Adam, choosing to ignore it, "minding our own business – well, minding our *sheep* – when this angel appears right in front of us."

"Like a piece of lightning," said Evie.

"I tell you something, he was tall!" said Adam.

"They are," said Jamie, nodding wisely. "Was it Gabriel? He stands at the right hand of God."

"Dunno," said Adam, "but he knew his stuff. Told us what had happened and where to find the baby."

"To you in Damon's town this day... " hummed Evie.

"*David's* town," corrected Adam, exasperated. "He told us about the manger and everything. And he told us to come and see. I mean – us! Ordinary us!"

They all looked at Jesus in silence, trying to grasp how they could be here, taking part in such an event.

"My dad says nobody's really up to all this amazing stuff," said Jamie. Adam and Evie nodded.

After a while longer of simply enjoying looking at the baby, they slid down off the bale.

"Bye bye, little lamb," Evie said to Jesus. "Night night, sleep tight. If the bugs bite, squash 'em."

Adam and Evie slipped out into the night, Evie trilling to herself something that sounded suspiciously like "Fa la la la la, la la la la" and Adam retorting "That makes no sense."

Jamie was left alone, kneeling by the side of the manger, leaning over. The baby opened his eyes and looked at Jamie for the very first time.

"Night night, Yeshi," whispered Jamie. "Welcome to our world."

Chapter Nineteen

FULFILLING SOME LAWS

Having ushered the Anointed One safely into the world, next on the to-do list was the registering of names – with the Romans, and with God.

Once Mary was rested, they took a gentle walk up the high street to the table where a bored scribe sat, flanked by a couple of soldiers. When they saw the newborn baby, people stepped aside and let them go to the front of the crowd so that Mary wouldn't have to stand for hours in the sun.

The scribe looked up at them, wondering when this job would end. He'd been pleased when he was assigned to Bethlehem; he had thought such a small, unimportant place couldn't have produced many people. He'd told his mum he'd be back in three or four days.

"Names?" he asked, willing himself to keep ploughing through.

"Peace be with you," said Joseph. "I'm Yosef Bar Ya'aqov, if you want it in the Hebrew."

"I don't," said the scribe.

"Right. I'm Joseph, son of Jacob. From the tribe of Judah. I'm of David's line."

"Who isn't?" sighed the scribe, rolling his eyes as he wrote it.

"This is my wife Mary, daughter of Eli, also descended from King David," Joseph continued. "Here we have James, son of Joseph." Jamie nodded to the scribe, a little nervous to exist suddenly, in the eyes of the Romans.

Joseph breathed deep and took a moment before the next bit. Jamie looked up and saw what it meant to him to claim the child as his own for the first time; tears glistened slightly on his eyelashes. "And the baby is Jesus, son of Joseph."

So there it was, official and out there. That is how he would be known – to everyone, unless his other identity became clear to them. If the Romans were compiling this mega-list of the whole empire to work out who they should keep an eye on, then that name should have been marked with asterisks and double-underlining and whatever the Romans used as highlighter – but the scribe put down his quill without noticing anything jaw-dropping had just happened.

"Pledge allegiance to Caesar Augustus," he said, already eyeing up the next in the crowd behind them.

"Just 'allegiance'?" asked Joseph cautiously. Leaders of great empires had a habit of declaring themselves to be gods and forcing everyone to worship them, which was *not* something any believing Jew was about to do. The Holy Writings were pretty specific that there was only one God, and that this was a big deal.

The scribe was fed up with the number of people who had queried this rather than just getting on with it and making his job quicker.

"Yes! Loyalty; obedience; goodwill. Warm regards will do."

Jamie wasn't sure they should do this, since they would be starting a rebellion in the next few years, but Joseph seemed comfortable with it.

"We wish the emperor well, and give him all the respect due to our earthly ruler," said Joseph.

"For now," added Jamie under his breath, making very sure the scribe and soldiers didn't hear.

"Good enough," the scribe said, giving them a small pottery disc stamped with a seal to prove they had been registered, and that was it. They could return to their crumbling tower, which was starting to feel like home, and the welcome of their assorted livestock roommates.

The baby yawned as they walked back, as if conducting official business on his first day of life had been a little tedious.

"There we are, Yeshi," Jamie told him. "You've got two daddies now!"

Over the next few days, the incomers there for the census gradually packed up and went, leaving room to breathe. The innkeeper got a nice room ready in her house, even finding a little cot, and they transferred their things. The donkey stayed with its new friends in the derelict tower, happy to have the extra space and nobody sleeping in their feeding trough.

Registering the baby's name with God was a much more dignified affair than the census had been. It happened on Shemini Atzeret, the eighth day of the Feast of Tabernacles, and people gathered at the inn for the ceremony. Jamie's family hadn't invited anyone they knew. Their friends and relatives would probably still be in the wrong place because of the census, or recovering at home from the disruption.

Jamie wouldn't have believed it possible to feel so at home among strangers. If anyone had told him beforehand that none of the people they cared about would be there, he would have thought it the worst disaster. Yet there was their kind innkeeper. There was her grandfather, sitting in the corner – who they could actually see and chat to at last, now the guests and their heap of cloaks had gone. There were Adam and Evie in their Sabbath best (the lamb waiting patiently outside), with their parents and as many uncles, aunts and cousins as weren't needed with the sheep right now. And there were other people Jamie had never met, brimming over with excitement at what the shepherds had told them just one short week ago. Was this not better than if it had happened in Nazareth, or even at Miriam's house? Jamie thought so. Everyone seemed to know exactly who this baby was and had come to mark a new life and hope beyond the usual celebration of a birth. There was no polite pretence of just another lovely baby naming: how moving, didn't the rabbi say it well and wasn't the mother's dress nice? As the local rabbi pronounced the name over the child, sealing his identity – Y'shua: Salvation of the Lord – many wept.

"He's a lovely little lamb," said Evie in satisfaction.

Somehow it felt as right as a trough for a royal bed, and unwashed shepherds as the welcoming committee to represent humanity. These people might be strangers, but Y'shua belonged to them as much as to his family; Jamie could see it in their faces. That unaccustomed feeling of humble wonder crept back into his heart.

They decided not to go back to Nazareth just yet. God's law said that all firstborn sons belonged to him, and must be brought to the Temple to be dedicated after they were forty days old. Given Mary's hard journey, there would have been no point in her traipsing all that way back – donkey, or no donkey – only to have to return a couple of weeks later! Much better to have a proper rest. And Joseph had no intention of leaving either her or little Yeshi, of course, so that meant they were all staying.

Jamie worried about how they would manage for money, away from work for so long.

"On the mountain of the Lord,... " Joseph reminded him. Joseph rightly guessed that a carpenter would be in demand in any small settlement where people's skills began and ended with sheep.

Their host's grandfather found a few tools to lend, as did Adam and Evie's dad, and Joseph and Jamie were kept busy – mending sheep pens, building sheep pens, making tables, fixing doors, mending more sheep pens...

There was great excitement when the time came to take Jesus to the Temple. They hadn't had chance to pack their nicest clothes when they'd set out on this journey in such a mad scramble, but they scrubbed themselves up as fresh and smart as they could. Messages had gone out to Miriam's family and Zechariah and Elizabeth about the baby's safe arrival, with an invitation to meet them at the Temple for the dedication, so Jamie couldn't wait to see them there.

They arrived into the bustle of Jerusalem through a different gate from their usual route, and Jamie quite liked the unaccustomed view and the feeling of living locally for a change. But the Temple still dominated, whichever way you approached, and a hushed excitement fell on the three of them as they brought this precious bundle up the wide steps to dedicate him to his heavenly Father.

The Temple wasn't packed as it would be close to a festival, though there were still some people around and enough mayhem to distract anyone trying to pray. Miriam was looking out for them. As soon as they arrived at the top and entered the Court of the Gentiles, she spotted them and dragged her parents over, closely followed by Zechariah and Elizabeth with baby John. The difference between the two families and their reactions to Jesus would not have been obvious to a passing stranger, but Jamie picked up on it right away. Miriam's family did everything you would expect – what anyone would do, greeting any other new baby – fussing; petting; cooing; exclaiming; begging to hold; kissing Mary; clapping Joseph on the back. Zechariah and Elizabeth simply stood there, choking back tears, barely able to keep from kneeling; unable to take their eyes from their King. Baby John was similarly transfixed, staring at his little cousin. He pointed a chubby finger at him.

"That's right, chicken," said Elizabeth softly, kissing her son. "We know who that is, don't we?"

Once the excitement had settled, Joseph looked to see which of the dove sellers had the shortest line.

"Off we go, then!" he said cheerfully, keeping up the pretence that this was just another dedication of just another baby.

Except that the baby's Other Father had very different ideas.

Chapter Twenty

WORTH THE WAIT

There was a disturbance over on the far side of the Court of the Gentiles as people split this way and that to let an old man come striding through, walking directly towards Mary, with purpose and fire in his eyes.

"Simeon!" said Matthan in surprise.

Simeon walked right up, without any hesitation or uncertainty, and took baby Jesus from Mary's arms. There was a gasp from people around. His behaviour had been strange enough, the way he'd pushed through without so much as an 'Excuse me' – but this? Take a baby from its mother's arms, when you didn't know the family and hadn't even asked permission? Dinah looked outraged, but Matthan tried to calm the situation.

"I'm sorry – he's usually such a godly man. He must have got confused."

He was about to return the baby to Mary when Zechariah put a hand on his arm to stop him. Mary herself was watching Simeon with no trace of distress, waiting to hear what he would say, sure that he must have been sent by God. People around the courtyard were stopping what they were doing to stare. Traders weren't dealing with their customers. Gentile families were curious. An electric silence fell. Jamie felt his heart pounding in anticipation.

Simeon looked at Jesus as if he were drinking him in. Every detail. In time, he nodded to himself.

"I can die now; yes, I can go in peace. You're releasing your servant, Sovereign Master. You've done what you promised me, and let me see the consolation of Israel – your Anointed One, your Christ."

Jamie was aware of the looks of sheer amazement all around – and the small clump of those right in the heart of it, including himself, who were not amazed at all.

Miriam turned to Jamie, her eyes round and wide.

"It's true," Jamie whispered.

"I just held him!" Miriam whispered back in awe. "I held him in my arms!" as if she couldn't believe that her small arms could possibly have contained the one who had come from ancient times.

Everyone in the Court of the Gentiles was listening now; even individuals who had been praying in the furthest colonnades were coming over.

"I've seen your saving grace!" Simeon went on, his voice becoming louder and more confident with every moment. He lifted the baby high and the people on all sides drifted closer, gazing at Jesus as if drawn to him. "The salvation you have prepared, now seen by all! A light to reveal truth and guide the way for the Gentiles. A light of glory for your people, Israel."

He lowered the child and smiled at Mary and Joseph.

"May the Lord bless you both," he said. "Bless you for your faithfulness and your great love of God."

He paused a moment, as if sensing new things now that he had delivered the first message, and spoke to Mary as if the others weren't there.

"This child will cause the falling and rising of many in the nation of Israel, you know. Oh yes – he's destined to be a sign which is spoken against, so that the thoughts of many hearts will be revealed."

He looked into Mary's face in the same hungry way he had done with Jesus, drinking from deep in her eyes, and a troubled expression crossed his faded features. "And a sword will pierce your own soul, too."

Most people weren't close enough to hear it, but those who were looked at Mary with concern. She and Simeon stared at each other, an unspoken sorrow reflecting back and forth between them in deepening waves which neither of them could understand.

There was a flurry near the gate that led to the Court of Women, as someone swept through. It was Anna, driven by the same fire they'd seen in Simeon's face. A murmur went around; she hadn't been seen in the outer court for many years! Others were following, not knowing why she'd told them to come: families, abandoning fellowship meals; pilgrims, leaving their sacrifices at the altar; even Levites and priests. Jamie spotted Reuben the friendly rabbi – watching Anna keenly, puzzled by her urgency, then understanding as soon as he caught sight of Mary.

Simeon handed the baby to Anna, and she also marvelled at what she was holding in her frail, human hands – too overcome to speak at first, then quickly too overcome *not* to speak.

"I praise you, God of our ancestors – God who made each one of us!" she cried out. "I thank you, loving Lord! That you should care about us, even though we wandered off like stupid sheep. That you should remember us and send a Rescuer!"

She looked around at the crowd.

"Who wants to be free? Who longs for the day when Jerusalem will be free? This is the one who will do it! He will break every chain and proclaim freedom for captives. He will buy us back from our enemy. From the greatest enemy of all! Our accuser will fall silent. On the day when this child is lifted up for all to see, Death itself will die."

She looked at the baby once more, his little face close to hers, with such love that Jamie's heart nearly burst. She kissed his brow tenderly, then returned him to Mary with a beautiful smile and walked back to the Court of Women. The people parted for her like a soft curtain that let her through and then covered her from sight. Likewise, Simeon passed through the crowd the other way, towards the entrance gate, and was gone.

No one wanted to rush back to what they'd been doing. Everyone was processing what they'd heard, in their own way, all loosely gathered around that clump of the baby's family and friends.

A seller of sheep and goats approached, more hesitant than those brash salespeople usually were.

"Would you like an offering? Take my finest."

Joseph remembered why they'd come; the dedication, of course! He tried to collect his thoughts, looking at the animals the seller was indicating. "Thanks, but we don't have much. We always give the smaller offering of doves or pigeons."

"There'd be no charge," said the seller.

"I know, and that's very kind of you," said Joseph, pressing his hand in gratitude. "But we have to follow our ancestor David's example, today of all days! We can't offer something to God which cost us nothing."

A dove seller came forward, equally uncertain; Joseph chose two and handed over the money. Then the small crowd walked with Jamie and his family towards the next court, as if they were bringing baby Y'shua to God on behalf of them all. Mary smiled her thanks to the people who weren't able to go further as they went through the gate. They reached the next one, and Mary took a moment to pray and give her darling Yeshi to God in her own heart before handing him to Jamie, since Joseph's arms were both full of dove. Jamie and the men passed into the Court of Israel, leaving Mary, Miriam and the other women watching through the gate.

The ceremony was a surprising mix of solemn and joyful. Being a very black-and-white sort of person, Jamie wasn't used to dallying in the greys, but it seemed appropriate for what we call a 'paradox': giving to God someone they firmly believed had come from God in the first place. Jamie started to wonder if *anything* they gave to God had really been theirs, or if they were just returning a sliver of what he'd already blessed them with – like when Jamie bought a Hanukkah gift for his dad

143

using money Joseph had given him.

When Jesus had been fully given over to his Father they brought him back to his mother and tried to take in all that had just happened.

Jamie remembered Anna. He wanted to tell her about the dedication and how *he* had been the one to hand the baby to the priest, so he looked around eagerly.

There she was, sitting over to one side – propped up against a pillar, face tilted skywards and eyes closed in prayer with that peaceful smile Jamie had seen so often.

He started towards her and the others came too, just as keen to share the moment with her. But partway Joseph abruptly held out his arm, barring them from going closer. Jamie looked at him in surprise – even more so when he saw the expression on his father's face. He looked wildly around the other adults; everyone was just as serious. Miriam clutched Jamie's arm – scared, wondering what was happening.

"What is it? What's the matter?" asked Jamie, wishing someone would say something.

"It's all right, sweetheart," said Elizabeth. "Don't be frightened. It's nothing to be sad about."

But the tears running down her cheeks made him doubt that very much. Mary clutched baby Jesus tightly and gave a sob.

There was a respectful hush across the court. Joseph and Zechariah moved towards Anna, looking carefully at her. Joseph knelt and took her hand; he touched her cheek, then her neck, and nodded briefly to the others.

"Is she... " Miriam ventured timidly.

"Yes," whispered Dinah. "She's gone."

"Oh dear. Oh dear," said Rabbi Reuben, choked up – finding as everyone does at such a time that there really are no words, and everything comes out stupidly trivial. "Oh dear, how sad."

"Elizabeth... " said Zechariah, removing his priestly

outer robe and handing it to Reuben, rolling up his sleeves. Elizabeth gave baby John to Dinah and went to join him.

"No – be careful, Zechariah," said Reuben as he realised what he intended. "You mustn't touch the body; you'll make yourself ceremonially unclean! You wouldn't be able to do your priestly duties for a while. Remember: a priest must prepare only his very closest relatives for burial."

"She trusted in the Lord as her husband and dedicated her life to him," said Zechariah. "She has no family left but him. This *is* my priestly duty. As the Lord's representative I am her closest relative, and we will take care of her now."

He took that tiny body into his arms, walking solemnly with Elizabeth to one of the side rooms – and that was the last Jamie ever saw of Anna, daughter of Phanuel, prophetess of the Living God.

Chapter Twenty-one

MICAH STRIKES AGAIN

Now that they had finished everything that needed to be done in Judea (or everything they *thought* needed to be done), Jamie and his family began to wind down their life in Bethlehem. They packed their things bit by bit – wondering, as is traditional, why they seemed to have more than they arrived with. Not including the baby, obviously; he was allowed to be an extra item.

One morning, when it looked as if they would be going within a day or two, Jamie went to Adam and Evie's house to say goodbye, taking some wooden toys Joseph had helped him make for them. Evie's gift was a lamb – recognisable in shape, if a little wonky around the nose – which she could carry everywhere and Jamie hoped might persuade her to put down the real thing. A forlorn hope; she liked it well enough, but her main interest seemed to be in showing it to her actual lamb (who also seemed to like it, as far as one could tell). She had no pockets and she couldn't manage both in her hands, so she quickly hit on carrying the alive-and-breathing lamb in her arms, and the wooden one in her teeth. Adam rolled his eyes in despair, though he did whisper to Jamie that maybe this would stop her interrupting him quite so often.

While they were sitting on the doorstep, with Jamie saying how in some ways he was looking forward to getting back home and in other ways he'd rather stay here, they noticed a dust cloud just outside Bethlehem.

It was a large cloud; bigger than ordinary travellers would make. A flock of sheep might make such a stir in the air, but the children would have heard bleating.

It drew closer, yet still they couldn't make out much, just tall shapes, swaying slowly and gracefully. It was a cloud filled with suspense. A tantalising cloud. The kind of cloud authors and filmmakers love to use in an attempt to whip you up into a frenzy of curiosity – just like I'm trying to do now – before the mist clears and you finally see the monster, or the alien, or the Edwardian gentleman from *The Railway Children* and Bobbie shouts "Oh! My Daddy, my Daddy!"

Or, indeed, the line of camels being ridden by the most dignified, stately, cultured, wealthy, exotic and mind-bogglingly impressive men you could ever imagine – because, yes, that is who it was.

Camels!!! These tall beasts with intriguing humps, looking down their thin noses with a permanent sneer, were so outside Jamie's experience he was nearly as astounded as when he saw the angels. And these *men* – covered in jewels and bright silks, far more noble than King Herod – who could they be, and why would they visit a sheep settlement like Bethlehem?

Jamie gasped, leaping to his feet. Why else would kingly people come, but to visit the King of kings?

Camels had not been on the list. Greeting wealthy foreign dignitaries had not been on the list. Jamie, Joseph and Mary may have carefully crossed off everything they thought was necessary before they left Bethlehem, but God had one more thing on the agenda.

The camel train entered the main street, and Jamie could see the exquisite detail of the men's clothes – and their hair and beards, which were oiled, curled and braided with gems. The imposing leader of the parade stopped and called to the children.

"Hail! We seek him who is born King of the Jews. We have seen his star in the east and are come hither, eagerly desirous to worship him, with reverence and awe."

"And/or what?" whispered Adam, but Jamie was too excited to explain.

"He's a lovely little lamb," Evie tried to tell the man,

but with the toy in her mouth it came out garbled. The stranger gazed blankly at her, thinking this must be one of the few languages he had not yet learnt.

It would have been Jamie's perfect chance to tell his story, bigging himself up to important people about how he was practically a prince and that he, alone of all boys, had been chosen to be brother of the king's King – but he was so overwhelmed by the dazzling newcomers, all he came out with was:

"I'll take you to him."

Arguably the most sensible thing he could have said, then or at any time over the next thirty-odd years.

He led them to the inn that wasn't a proper hotel and watched them dismount. Camels, it turned out, were more accommodating than horses, for all their haughty faces; each one knelt for its rider to disembark. Jamie would normally have found that very interesting, but right now his brain was too fried to take it in.

The men brushed dust from their robes and smoothed their hair, regarding the house with interest.

"Not a royal palace," observed one. "An humble dwelling."

"It is fitting, perhaps," said another. "The god of Belteshazzar, who did lead us here and who is forever to be praised, has graciously presenced his chosen one amongst common persons. His wisdom is not like unto our wisdom."

They all nodded, making "Mmm" noises like a cow.

Jamie only understood what they were saying enough to grasp vaguely that they had called him common, but he was in no fit state to object. Staring at their silks and jewels, and smelling the fine fragrance that wafted from them, he felt quite grubby. He became painfully aware that his tunic had not been washed since the last time he had used his sleeve as a hanky.

One of them beckoned a boy, following on foot with

a long stick to prod the camels in the right direction. He was tall and handsome, and seemed a very big boy to Jamie, nearly twice his age. Although he was carrying out a servant's task, he was dressed nearly as richly as the men and looked as if he knew (and cared about) the difference between his sleeve and his handkerchief when it came to blowing his nose. The boy opened a saddle bag and produced an intricate casket made of pure gold, a carved alabaster box of the kind used to hold perfumed incense, and another of black marble.

The men took the beautiful containers – each a work of art – and looked at each other, overwhelmed by the importance of the moment. Then they nodded to Jamie, who stepped shakily to the door and opened it.

As he stepped into the dimness of the inn's main room, he saw that Mary was sitting with Jesus on her lap, singing softly to him, while Joseph gathered the tools they had been lent, ready to return them. The innkeeper busied herself with washing up the breakfast things and her grandfather dozed in his chair. Jamie cleared his throat to get their attention – another great opportunity for a speech that would be remembered down the ages, but all he could say was:

"Some visitors."

Joseph came and stood by Mary, both wondering who might have been drawn to see the child this time. Jamie stepped aside to allow the strangers in, and they moved as one towards the little family. The innkeeper's mouth fell open when she saw them, but Mary and Joseph smiled at them with the same quiet, unsurprised joy as when they greeted the shepherds.

The men knelt and placed the elaborate, costly items on the floor in front of Jesus. Were they *giving* them to him? Then each of them laid face down, completely flat, with their arms stretched out towards him. Jamie saw through the open door that, out in the dusty street, the boy was doing the same.

They stayed like that in silence for what felt like forever, then outside one of the camels made a snort of protest. The boy leaped up guiltily, and the innkeeper also sprang to life, going out to him. Jamie followed, partly to help and partly because there were so many questions he wanted to ask this boy who behaved like a servant yet looked like a prince.

"Sorry. So sorry, dear. You'll want to feed and water your... camels," said the innkeeper breathlessly, obviously as unused to such beasts as Jamie was. "See that old tower there? Well, not much of a tower now, but the ground floor's just about all right. Pop them in there. Wait a min, let me just get you more hay."

The boy bowed to Jamie as he waited for her return. Jamie bowed back nervously, a little surprised at the formality and very much aware of the small crowd gathering to stare at the camels.

"Hello," he said to the boy. "Are you kings?"

"My masters are Magi – wise and learned ones, from Babylon, far to the East. I myself am an apprentice Magus, whom they teach in all the skills and knowledge of the ages."

"Oh," said Jamie, considerably more nervous. "I'm a carpenter myself. My name's Jamie."

"My name is Ahura Zaramanah Asha Hu-Raoda Vanhu-Barezan Bagahada-Putha," said the apprentice Magus.

Jamie looked at him, the cogs of his brain whirring, trying to catch hold of a sound he might have a chance of reproducing.

"Translated into the Greek, that is Sopho Meletimeno Polikalos Omorpho Ekpliktika-Psilo Theodoropoulos," said the apprentice Magus.

Jamie's mouth opened and closed a few times, but nothing came out.

"So you can call me Theo," said Theo.

"Hello, Theo!" said Jamie, brightening. "Welcome to Bethlehem."

"Bet Lechem: 'House of Bread'," nodded Theo, giving the correct Hebrew pronunciation and looking round appreciatively. "Also known as Ephrath."

He wasn't showing off. Having the Magi teach him all the knowledge of the ages, day in, day out, seemed to have made him think such learning was natural.

The innkeeper reappeared, lugging some hay bales.

"Here you are, dear," she gasped. "And will you – will you be staying, do you think?" Her voice squeaked upwards at the idea of such important guests, and yet she knew they were hardly likely to have a quick snack and a comfort break then head back home to Babylon.

"That would be appreciated in great measure, madam," said Theo, bowing to her.

She gave a little curtsey in return, her voice rising a few more strangled notches in panic.

"Perfect. Give me a sec; I'll get some rooms ready."

"For my masters, solely," Theo assured her. "I myself will be content to couch me in the straw, where lie the animals."

"Lovely," she said and scurried back into her house.

Jamie helped Theo carry the hay bales to the broken-down tower, the camels stalking gracefully beside them.

The innkeeper's animals and the donkey were startled as the camels entered, not sure if they approved or not, and hesitant to make eye contact – a little like somebody who has never met anyone from a different country before; wishing to be polite, but not sure what to expect. The camels looked down on the domestic animals with pity, aware of their own glamour.

Jamie and Theo drew water from the nearby well to refill the drinking trough, although the camels seemed more interested in the hay and having their saddles taken off. Theo explained that camels could store water for a long time; that's what their humps were for. Jamie was fascinated, imagining (wrongly) the humps to be hollow, like the inside of a leather bottle, and wondering if he'd be able to hear the water swishing around.

As they filled the feeding trough, it brought back a flood of memories for Jamie. He told Theo that the baby they had travelled so far to see had been born right here, and that this manger had been his first bed.

"Migdal Eder!" exclaimed Theo, looking eagerly around at the rough stone walls. "Of course."

Jamie stared, wondering what on earth he meant.

"It means 'Tower of the Flock'" explained Theo, "and verily has it stood here since the time of your fathers."

"David?" said Jamie. "He looked after his dad's sheep in Bethlehem, before he was king."

"Your father David, yes," admitted Theo, "but longer yet than he. Your father Jacob, also, sojourned here and did pitch his tents – him and his sons – in the very fields beyond this tower."

Jamie felt a shiver of excitement. Had they slept in a building that had been known by Jacob and his family, nearly two thousand years before?

"'Tis a sad tale," said Theo. "They reached this spot following hard upon the death of Rachel, his favoured wife, taken too soon. Jacob mourned her here."

"I know her!" said Jamie, glad that at least he could remember something. "She was Joseph's mother – him with the coat of many colours – and Benjamin's mother – and Jacob loved her very much."

"That is true," said Theo, smiling at his enthusiasm. "You have studied well. Rachel is founding mother to many of your people; a matriarch of the nation. But this Migdal Eder, built to watch o'er the flocks of shepherds long since gone... This is that very tower of which the prophet Micah spoke."

Him again! Jamie listened in astonishment as Theo laid his hand on the crumbling wall in awe.

"It precedes that passage of renown in which proclaims he: 'Yet thou, Bethlehem Ephrathah, notwithstanding that thou art so teeny weeny... '"

Jamie was a little thrown at the choice of words. Theo spoke Jamie's language superbly – better than Jamie himself, though in such a strangely old-fashioned way – but clearly his vocabulary had sometimes been picked up from odd sources. Jamie tried to concentrate.

"Merely a moment before does this same Micah state that the very kingdom shall come, and your god's lordship be restored, in Migdal Eder."

The *building?* Micah had predicted not just the village, but the actual *building* where it would happen? Jamie felt he had not done this guy's prophetic powers justice, and that if Theo were to tell him Micah had also stated the height of the donkey and what colour underwear Joseph would be wearing, he would feel inclined to believe it.

"I devoured his writing last night, upon my bed, and yet I understood it not, till now," mused Theo. "We had been informed yestereve of the Ephrathine prophecy that did lead us here this day – and so, naturally, I wished to search the scripture for myself."

"Naturally," agreed Jamie, thinking that nothing would persuade him to pick a Hebrew scroll as some light bedtime reading. "But why did you come in the first place? How did you know? What brought you here?"

"A star," said Theo.

Chapter Twenty-two
STARRY, STARRY DAY

The two boys sat cross-legged on the floor of that very room where Jesus had been born – looking through the open door over those very fields where Jacob and his family had camped – and Theo told his whole story.

"The Magi have studied the night skies these many centuries, plotting the heavenly lights and seeking to understand their times and movements. There are the stars, which sweep majestically across our sky each night, while fixed remaining in their patterns. And then there are the planets, the wanderers, which weave a dance and remain not constant. We observe them all, and carefully record our sightings. Now, understand that my people had watched most keenly these twenty years or more, knowing that the Lord your god's anointed one was destined to come soon."

"I – *what?*" shrieked Jamie, frightening the donkey and making the camels stop chewing. "What do you mean, you knew?"

"It is in the writings of Belteshazzar, greatest of all the Magi," said Theo. "Your prophet Daniel, the young Jewish nobleman carried off to exile in Babylon when probably of an age with me."

Jamie stared in disbelief. He knew about Daniel; that scroll had some of his favourites! Clop always fought the other boys at school for the chance to translate it. People being hurled into fiery furnaces and dens of hungry lions; a king eating grass like a donkey; a finger appearing in mid-air *without a body attached* and writing on a wall – what was not to love? But Jamie couldn't remember it saying "Oh, and by the way – this is when Messiah will come."

Theo was puzzled. "Have not your leaders also been watching, now that the time draws nigh?"

"Not so's you'd notice," said Jamie.

"Belteshazzar, your prophet Daniel, was given a message from the Lord your god, by one Gabriel."

"Ha!" shouted Jamie. The camels looked over in disapproval. "Sorry. Carry on."

"The messenger did say unto him that the time of 'mashiach nagid', or 'anointed and princely one' – would arrive seven sevens and sixty-two sevens from the giving of the command to restore Jerusalem. That is four hundred and eighty-three."

Maths was not Jamie's strong point, beyond the cost of one plank, two planks, three planks, so he was happy to take Theo's word for it.

"Then, within but one seven more would be achieved the ending of sin and atoning for wickedness. Now, from the directions and moneys given to Ezra the priest, to re-establish the city as a civic power, unto this present time, is four hundred and fifty-three years. The time of mashiach the prince, therefore, is thirty years from now."

(I won't interrupt to explain how I've reckoned that – the camels would be cross with me. I'll put an extra bit at the end of the book, if you really want to know!)

Jamie was as astounded as a modern American would be if they found out that Christopher Columbus had predicted, in his twenties, that *Frozen 2* would hit the big screen precisely four hundred and eighty-three years after the city of Buenos Aires was founded.

Let's try another one: Jamie was as every bit as gob-smacked as someone in Britain today would be if they heard that Richard the Third, at the age of six, had announced that *Harry Potter and the Prisoner of Azkaban* would be published exactly four hundred and eighty-three years after the birth of Henry the Eighth's daughter Mary, the first queen to rule England.

Would an Australian example make it clearer? Jamie was as flabbergasted as... Look, the point is, Daniel had lived a *very* long time before, so the idea he could have known something that would happen in Jamie's day was *extremely* surprising. And in these silly, made-up illustrations, Columbus and King Richard were even using future events as the *start* of their countdowns; things they couldn't have known would happen, because they didn't until nearly sixty years after!

Jamie's mind was swimming. What had Rabbi Asher been *doing*, not telling them about this? Had *nobody* noticed, except a bunch of star-gazing, maths-obsessed scholars in an eastern corner of the empire?

Theo watched Jamie wrestling to come to terms with it, wondering if he had grasped it now.

"Therefore you see," he went on, "you should expect a happening of great import around the time your brother attains the age of thirty."

"Right," said Jamie, gulping. An objection occurred to him. "Though we'll have it sorted by then. Daniel's a bit out in his dates; it'll be more like twenty years when we throw out the Romans and Herod and everyone."

"The prophet is clear," insisted Theo. "Thirty years more unto the time of the anointed one, and after that, shall he be cut off and have nothing."

"Who, Messiah? Well, that's definitely wrong!" said Jamie. "He's not going to be cut off, he's going to win a great victory and rule on David's throne forever."

"He is," agreed Theo. "But he shall also be cut off."

"How? They can't both be true."

"I know not," said Theo. He didn't seem the least bit bothered that he knew not (sorry; that he didn't know) – which struck Jamie as an unsatisfactory attitude from someone who claimed to be learning the knowledge of the ages. Although, since it was Daniel's prophetic superpowers that had brought Theo all this way and

156

turned out to be spot on, Jamie supposed he couldn't be surprised at his level of trust.

"So. You were looking at the sky," he said, wanting to know about the star.

"We were," said Theo. "And I must tell you, son of Joseph, I have seen many wonders this two years since! The planet you know as Jupiter drew nigh unto that which is called Saturn, not once, not twice but *thrice!* Within but half a year. This is a very great wonder."

It didn't sound particularly wondrous to Jamie. He'd noticed nothing special himself over the last two years.

"Ordinary stars?" he checked. "Those tiny pin pricks in the sky?"

"But in extraordinary places," explained Theo.

"Closer together; yeah, you said," Jamie pouted with dissatisfaction. "I thought you were going to say they lit up the sky like a fireball! I've seen angels."

He told him all about it, but Theo remained just as excited by the signs he had seen, going full-on science geek.

"That is indeed a wonder – yet is not the planning and drawing together of natural events across centuries of circling years equally to be marvelled at?" he enthused. "My masters calculate this triple twinning would happen but once in a *millennium!* And *then*, in but a short space thereafter – then the planet Mars did join them! The three conjoined in such proximity as may only be seen every *eight hundred* years! Not only had we witnessed two such rarities within our lifetime; it was all in a matter of some nine months. Do not you see, son of Joseph? Unusual shenanigans in the heavenly realms! The Lord your god had spake his word unto Belteshazzar in days long past, which alerted your servants to await a sign in our time. Your servants, seeing these heavenly shenanigans, believed that the time was indeed nigh. And then did grow upon us the notion that, perchance, if the mighty god of

157

Belteshazzar had vouchsafed – "

"Sorry, what?"

" – had *allowed* us to understand these things, might not he also graciously permit us to journey here and pay homage to the newborn king? Else wherefore would he acquaint us with the tidings? We did humbly hope to see this new era dawn with our own eyes."

Jamie was stirred by Theo's excitement. They'd read that Messiah would light up some Gentiles, and here Theo was, right in front of him, face aglow. So soon! Y'shua didn't even look impressive yet, or have a horse to ride, and already he was having such a deep effect.

"We beseeched the Lord your god to reveal to us the due season to set out, if so he willed it," Theo continued. "Belteshazzar named him 'revealer of mysteries', and so he is. He sent a star – a guest star, one not seen before. A broom or tailèd star; a comet, as you know them. It appeared in the east at its first rising, and we *knew* it was for us he sent it. He kindly beckoned us to join the hootenanny – shindig – party, for his baby king!"

"When was this?" asked Jamie, agog.

"In the spring, a few weeks after the moon's soft light was turned to deepest red. I mean the first such event this year, not that which did but recently befall."

"It's happened twice this year?" asked Jamie in amazement. "The one a few weeks ago was the night little Yeshi was born!"

"Indeed?" said Theo. "The prior was a six-month before, at the time your people celebrate the Passover."

Jamie was beside himself with excitement. "That's when his cousin was born! His cousin who's going to be the prophet who clears the way for him! Did the moon go all pink for *both* of them?"

"You see now, son of Joseph?" laughed Theo. "You understand the thrill of watching heaven's wonders? We will make a star-struck scholar of you yet."

"So is that when you set out, when you saw the star

with the tail?"

"Prepared we for a long journey," said Theo, "and in due course began. Upon the way my masters bought frankincense made by those who best know how to blend fine perfumes. Also myrrh. The gold is of Ophir, the best and purest, as befits a king. Finally reached we the beautiful land, the one your people wept for in their exile by Babylon's waters. Ancestral home of Daniel, and his city of Jerusalem. That was our aim."

"Jerusalem?" said Jamie, a little surprised. These Magi had missed it, for all their wisdom.

"We knew not of the Ephrathine prophecy till yesterday!" Theo reminded him.

Jamie had never heard anyone call 'But-you-Bethlehem-Ephrathah' the Ephrathine prophecy before. He suspected his friend might have invented a new theological phrase. (By which I mean I think *I* might have invented a new theological phrase. Cool. Let's work it into conversation and confuse people!)

"I am persuaded your own wise ones have been looking to Bethlehem for long ages past," said Theo.

Ah. Jamie had forgotten that his people, too, had not been *quite* across all the facts. Rabbi Asher, in particular, had been sleeping on the job.

"It seemed most meet – fitting – to us that a great king should be born in a palace," explained Theo. "That is earthly wisdom, is it not? That would be a reasoned expectation. And, thus, made we our way unto the dwelling of King Herod and requested audience."

"Herod!" gasped Jamie. "You went to his palace?"

"Yea, and moreover he did invite us in, with much civility, pomp and ceremony."

Jamie looked blank.

"Bling," said Theo. "His delight was great at a visit from afar. After choice refreshment, presented he my masters with gifts of spicèd oils, finest silks and much cool stuff. I stood at a distance, attentive with the bag, ready to offer up our gifts for the baby king. But soon transpired it that no such infant lay within those walls."

"Too right!" said Jamie, indignant at the thought of Yeshi being linked to Herod – then remembering he'd also wished they could go to such a palace when it was time for him to be born.

An important point hit him. "You didn't give him any of our presents, did you? I mean, my brother's."

"Fear not!" laughed Theo. "Herod appeared non-plussed – puzzled – as we inquired concerning the newborn king of the Jews. Then judged we all mashiach was not here. As my masters called for the gifts, they threw me looks of caution and alarums. I dug deep, and – the gods be thanked – I grasped the scented pomade with which my elder master oils his beard, the embroidered linen sash upon which he wipes the comb, and plush velvet cloth of purple for the drying of feet. Herod was mightily pleased to receive them. Needs must we purchase more at earliest opportunity."

Jamie was impressed with Theo's cheek – to present King Herod with some beard oil and a couple of used towels from a Magi wash bag.

"Herod did feast us richly, though he knew naught of the royal babe," continued Theo. "Enquiring of his learnèd men, he was diligent and most keen to find out all he could to aid us in our search. Then slept we sound, on silken sheets. We rose betimes – early – and, oh, what should greet us in the dusk before the dawn? It was our star again! Our special star, wandered in its natural course to southern skies, directly o'er the place mashiach king, the christ-child, lay."

"It led you here?" breathed Jamie, filled with awe.

"It *pointed* to him!" said Theo. "The tail stretched up, the head directly down. And thus it went ahead of us, till rosy-fingered dawn did sweep it from the sky."

160

Chapter Twenty-three

IMMANUEL

The boys' stomachs soon reminded them it was past lunchtime, so they trekked the short distance back to the centre of Bethlehem and the innkeeper's food. They passed Joseph on the way, taking the Magi to show them where Jesus was born.

"Migdal Eder!" Jamie heard one say, and the others nodded, going "Mmmm." Joseph looked as perplexed as Jamie had – clearly in for the same explanation.

The innkeeper was hot and bothered, having just had to rustle up a meal out of nowhere for people who had dined the night before at Herod's palace, but Theo assured her it smelled delicious. (He said 'delectable', but Jamie thought that was probably what he meant)

Mary had just given Yeshi his lunch too, rocking him against her, patting his back. When the boys finished eating, she suggested that Theo and Jamie might like to take over while she had a nap. Jamie took the cloth she'd draped across her shoulder and put it over his own, since jiggling a baby about shortly after it has been fed is not without risk. He leant little Yeshi against his chest and they went outside to the yard behind the inn.

Once the contents of the tiny tummy had settled, one way or another, they laid him on the ground so that he could kick about. He enjoyed that, and gurgled with pleasure as Theo dangled the silver bells on the end of his silken belt for him to grab.

Theo believed this birth had eternal importance and that it was extraordinary he'd even heard about it, since he was not of Jacob's line and knew little of Daniel's god. He had expected to worship respectfully from afar, if he was allowed to worship at all. Jamie could see how the wonder of it consumed him – that he could be this close and share these simple, intimate moments, and yet still adore with all the reverence he felt due to one who had come from ancient times to reign forever. A mystery this unknown god of Daniel seemed to specialise in revealing, just as he'd said.

The innkeeper poked her head out of the back door. "Immanuel," she sighed, seeing Theo play with Jesus.

"Yes, that's it!" said Theo, as he translated it in his mind. "God is fully 'with us' indeed."

"How long do you think you'll be staying, dear?"

"My masters will decide," he replied, "but I'll warrant not long. Tonight only, perchance. We must return to Herod. In faith, our duty was to hasten thither ere now."

"They should have gone back to Herod already," Jamie translated for the innkeeper; his brain was starting to tune in to the way Theo spoke.

"Righty ho," said the innkeeper breezily, as rising panic glazed her eyes again. She disappeared inside, trying not to think about her guests getting another chance to compare her food and bedding with Herod's.

"We're probably going tomorrow too," said Jamie. "You were lucky you caught us."

Theo laughed. "I used to think the gods of luck the mightiest of all. But could luck account for the timings of our journey, or the calculations of Belteshazzar?"

"You'd have to be very, *very* lucky," agreed Jamie. "Why are you going back to Herod?"

"He did instruct my masters to return straightway with news of the child, so that he also may come and worship him."

Jamie's eyes widened. A visit from the *king!* Of course, Jamie's brother was going to be a king too, and a much more important one – but he wasn't yet. And of course, Herod was vile – but maybe he would be nice to them if he knew that they were royalty like him? *Obviously,* there would come a time when Jamie and his brother would throw Herod out – or Herod would realise their superior claim and resign – but in the meantime, wouldn't it make all those people who'd been horrible sit up and take notice, if Jamie met the king?

"I'll tell Dad we'd best not leave yet," said Jamie. "I wonder if Herod has any grandchildren our age? They might like to meet Yeshi too, and we could play."

"Have a care, son of Joseph," said Theo, seeing all Jamie's dreams of being invited to sleepovers at the palace flitting across his face. "Caesar has said – and said well – it is better to be Herod's pig than his son."

"Why?" asked Jamie in surprise. He didn't know quite the kind of thing he expected a Roman emperor to say, but that wasn't it.

"I take his meaning to be that a pig would face less danger of slaughter," said Theo.

"Has Herod... killed his son?" whispered Jamie, as if Herod's spies might be hiding in the laundry pile.

"More than one," said Theo grimly, "and diverse other family members, not least his favourite wife – even her mother. Your former king; many priests and rabbis; half your holy council, and many other persons of no fame the chronicles might record. *Any* he believes may threat his rule. Be not flattered by his friendship; his only constancy is to those in power above him."

They spent a lovely evening with the Magi, Adam and Evie and their parents. Even the ever-flustered innkeeper took some time to relax and eat with them, and her grandfather and the oldest Magus swapped tall tales of the glory days. Then they had an early night, as there were long journeys to begin the next day.

It wasn't much after dark when Jamie heard a rattling at the window shutter. It only disturbed him because he slept on the opposite side of the room to his family these days, since the baby was liable to wake more times during the night than Jamie felt was reasonable.

He was rolling over to block it out, when there came a hoarse whisper:

"James, son of Joseph! Wakest thou?"

Then knocking on the shutters further along, where the Magi slept.

Jamie stumbled out of bed into the main room of the inn, unlocking the door to Theo, who was shaking and out of breath. One of the Magi came from his room in a dressing gown of silk brocade.

"What is it, Sopho Meletimeno Polikalos Omorpho Ekpliktika-Psilo Theodoropoulos?" he whispered.

"My master, I had a dream this night," gasped Theo.

"Tell me your dream and I will use my skills and arts to interpret it."

"As I lay upon my bed of straw, a messenger from the god of Belteshazzar did appear unto me – "

"Gabriel?" asked Jamie eagerly.

"I know not. He bade us not to call upon King Herod, but rather return to our land by another way."

"Oh. The interpretation is fairly clear," said the Magus, a little disappointed. "Make haste, we must waken the others."

The Magi dressed hurriedly, and Jamie helped Theo load the bags onto the camels, which he had brought with him from the old tower.

"We will head east, towards Qumran," whispered the Magus. "Beyond, may we cross the Jordan, and thence to Arabia." He handed Jamie a small velvet bag filled with coins. "For our hostess, with heartfelt gratitude. Come, let us depart!"

As the Magi mounted their camels, Theo bowed solemnly to Jamie.

"Farewell, James, son of Joseph, brother of mashiach king. I return to my land a different way in more than mere geography, with much to think on. May the god of your fathers and of Daniel ever guard and guide you."

"Farewell, Theo Doppy Poppalos," said Jamie, also bowing. "Safe journey."

He watched until the dust kicked up by the camels'

hooves, which had revealed the king-like strangers only that morning, hid them again under the starry sky.

Eventually he went back to his room; there was no point standing in the street now his friend had gone. He fully intended to cuddle up under the covers and doze straight off, but as he entered, Joseph was calling out in his sleep. Mary was awake, watching him with concern.

"Dad too?" whispered Jamie. "Theo just had a dream. They've had to go."

"I wonder if we will," said Mary, picking up little Jesus and holding him close. "He said something about Herod. And Egypt."

Egypt? Jamie barely had time to think about this before Joseph sat bolt upright, suddenly awake. He looked at them, quickly processing the situation and seeing that they had already half-guessed. He hugged Mary, giving her a kiss to reassure her.

"Come on. We need to go."

"To *Egypt?*" asked Jamie in amazement.

"Yes," said Joseph. "The Lord led Jacob and his family to Egypt to keep them safe, and now he's leading us. Dress quickly in your darkest clothes and let's gather our things."

"Why do we need to be kept safe?" asked Mary, suspecting she knew but wanting to face the worst. She looked steadily at Joseph, forcing him to tell her.

"Herod wants to kill Yeshi," said Joseph. "But God sent the angel to warn us. He's looking after us."

Jamie didn't even think of asking which angel it was; this was getting serious. Mary nodded, unable to speak.

It didn't take long, as they'd already packed. All they had to do was decide what they couldn't carry, now that they were travelling in a hurry. When people have to flee from sudden danger, even today, they leave most of their old life behind.

Sadly, this included the Magi's gifts, which were way too heavy. Jamie could hardly bear to leave them, though he trusted the innkeeper to keep them safe. He hoped maybe one day they'd be able to collect them.

"It's only stuff," Joseph comforted him. "Things."

But inside the gold casket they found many coins; they could certainly take them.

Mary held Jesus against herself and starting binding him to her with cloths, so her hands would be free. That's how she often carried him, to travel or work – but Joseph drew close, speaking in an undertone.

"Better not. We need to be able to pass him quickly between us." Mary looked at him, puzzled, and Jamie strained his ears, wondering what his father meant. "In case something happens to one of us," Joseph added.

Joseph divided the Magi's money equally between the three of them, tucking it safely into their belts.

"Just in case we get separated for a little while," he said lightly, as if it was no big deal – but Jamie had heard what he said to Mary. The brave, confident boy was too scared to move as he realised his father thought it was possible that Jamie might have to carry on alone.

Joseph saw his fear and knelt in front of him, squeezing his hands. "God is with us."

They strapped their belongings securely to their backs and Mary held Jesus tightly as they left the room. Joseph put payment for the innkeeper by the fireplace, so Jamie rested the Magi's velvet purse next to it. Then they slipped out into the night.

"Shall I fetch the donkey?" whispered Jamie.

"No," replied Joseph, "we'll have to leave it. We can't risk the roads. The angel said Herod would search for Y'shua. We have to go up over the hills, by rocky passes and deserted ways. Let's go."

Chapter Twenty-four

RACHEL'S TEARS

They crossed the open fields beyond Bethlehem as quickly as they could – aware that anyone might look out of a window and see them – taking the shortest route to the start of the hills, where the ground was rougher and they wouldn't stand out so much.

Then they began to climb. It was hard work, if you avoided the sheep paths which always took the best way. Thirsty work, too, but water is heavy, so they hadn't brought any. The darkness was double-edged; it gave some protection from others seeing them, yet it made the broken hillside treacherous.

At first they could walk upright, even though it was often steep, but sometimes they reached places where they had to clamber with their hands as well as their feet. Whenever that happened, they got into a rhythm of someone going up a little ahead, then the next person, then the one at the bottom passing the baby up till he reached the top – then the other two climbing past so that he could be handed up again. Those parts were slow and painstaking, like rock climbers tied to each other, gradually edging further up. But they kept at it and steadily made progress until, once more, they were at a part where they could walk again.

Jamie was nearly at the pass that would take them over the side of this hill and out of sight of the village, with Joseph coming up behind, carrying Jesus, when they heard a muted call from Mary. She was stuck a little further down in a gully, as thorns had tangled up in her long robe and around her foot. Joseph saw that she couldn't get free, pulling and kicking at them with no effect as she tried to keep her balance, gripping the rocks with her other hand.

"Here, take Yeshi," he whispered. "I'll help her."

Jamie scrambled back down to him and took the baby. Joseph quickly reached Mary, leaning around her as he pulled the thorns and hacked at them with a knife. Jamie watched, aware of his heart thumping. Aware of Yeshi's tiny heart, too, and that warmth, and weight, and slight wriggliness of a real baby that no doll can match. Everybody's hopes – all the visions of freedom that kept people alive long past their time just to catch a glimpse of it, or caused them to travel for months because an unknown god had called to them – all of it, here in Jamie's arms, wrapped up in this one snuffly bundle.

A distant scream shattered the night.

Jamie nearly yelled out with the shock, and Joseph and Mary grabbed on to each other to keep from falling. The distance didn't make it any less piercing; it went through their souls. They looked down to Bethlehem, where they thought they saw activity. Lamps and torchlight. Someone running? The woman screamed again, then it turned to the most distraught, inconsolable sobbing Jamie had ever heard.

Joseph whispered urgently up to Jamie.

"Go! Run as fast as you can and don't stop. Keep running, whatever happens!"

Jamie froze, staring down at Bethlehem and the terrified faces just below him. More screams from more women. Shouts from men. More running. And all ending in those wrenching sobs.

"Go!" pleaded Mary with every ounce of strength she could muster, and Jamie sprang to life.

He turned to face the narrow pass on the shoulder of the hill and threw himself towards it with everything he had, clutching the baby to his chest and running up the jagged slope in the near darkness, never slowing to get his balance, never feeling to choose the best way, never stopping when he stumbled forwards and skinned his

168

knees – and never, *ever* for one moment losing his grip on the child in his arms.

The baby started to whimper, upset at the sudden shaking about.

"It's all right, Yeshi. It's all right. Shhhhh shh shh. Good boy," Jamie gasped between breaths, desperate for him not to cry.

He broke through the pass to the other side and skidded for about thirty feet down a steep slope of loose stones and pebbles he hadn't expected to be there, falling backwards as his feet shot from under him and sliding the last part in a lying position.

At least now he was out of sight of the village and there was level ground for a while. He scrambled to his feet and pounded along, each breath stabbing his lungs more sharply the longer he went. He hardly even noticed the stitch in his side or the cramp in his legs, but when bitter-tasting bile kept coming up into his mouth he had to stop for a moment to be sick.

As he wiped his mouth, about to continue, he heard Joseph and Mary running up behind. Mary grabbed Y'shua almost roughly, squeezing him to her, collapsing to her knees, wracked with a silent version of the same sobs which had torn the hills.

"What was it?" Jamie asked, shocked by the horror on his father's face.

"Herod's men," panted Joseph, bent double in pain and grief. "They killed the babies."

It was true. All the little boys under two years old, from Bethlehem and the area around it. Herod the Great, who craved a fame that would continue far beyond his own time – little did he know it, but he made certain his name would never be forgotten with one casual decision that will outlive any monument of stone. His buildings rivalled the Seven Wonders of the World, but they will crumble. Many have already. Yet this one act, against a handful of little ones whose names we don't even know, will last – to his memory, and theirs.

As Jamie stood there, trying to catch his breath and hearing that terrible sorrow echoing faintly in the distance, something prodded him to remember a passage from the synagogue school. Where was it from; Jeremiah? He was usually the sad one.

"There's a voice crying in the hills," recited Jamie. "It's Rachel, weeping for her children. She's sad and she won't be comforted, because they aren't any more."

Mary and Joseph calmed in their gasping for air to think of this, as the mourning of however many Rachels, mothers of Israel, went up like an offering of precious incense.

Joseph nodded, remembering it. "But a little after that, God says Rachel will be comforted, one day. He says a new time is coming. A new promise." He gently helped Mary back up. "We need to keep going. It's because of things like this he sent Y'shua."

They trudged on.

"Aren't we safe now?" asked Jamie. "Couldn't we sleep, or at least rest a bit?"

"We must get well past Herodium," said Joseph. "It's one of his fortresses, and it's on that big hill to our left. He might have sent a message to his guards there too. We can't risk it; we have to stay quiet and keep off the paths. If we walk through the night, we should make it to Hebron; we can rest there."

Jamie felt a little comforted at the thought. They had friends there who would care for them; they could tell them of the horrors of this night. They wouldn't feel so alone. The thought of a big hug from Elizabeth, and Zechariah's quiet strength, spurred him on through the long night. Not just Jamie; he noticed that Mary, too,

170

was walking with more hope, her eyes fixed ahead. She'd made this journey once before in difficult times, carrying Jesus in a very different way long before anyone could have known it by looking at her. She had trusted then that the elderly couple would give her shelter and support, and there was no doubt in her mind that they would do so again.

As the night wore on, they still didn't speak much but they felt able to stop occasionally and drink at a stream. Mary gradually let her fierce grip on Jesus loosen, and allowed the others to take turns with her to carry him.

As it drew close to dawn, Jamie was so wobbly he was afraid he might not make it in time. He gritted his teeth and forced himself to keep going, but his legs were so much shorter and all his scabs and bruises stung. He knew he was slowing them down.

Then he saw a shape in the dark, slightly to one side. Smaller than a tree. Thinner than a rock. Less bushy than a bush. At first it seemed still, but then it gave a shake in a way that seemed reassuringly familiar. Jamie went over to investigate and found their very own donkey, waiting patiently for them!

"What are you doing?" hissed Joseph, as Jamie and the donkey nuzzled each other with joy.

"It's the donkey!" Jamie whispered back. "We've met up with the road, and here it is, just standing here!"

How it had got free – whether Theo had loosened it by mistake, or on purpose; or the innkeeper; or an angel; or it just randomly happened – and by what heightened sense of sight or smell, or instinct, or miracle, it had come the right way – it was all a mystery, but one they were very grateful for.

"'On the mountain of the Lord, it will be provided,'" said Jamie, his arms round its lovely warm neck.

"I never heard anyone teach it could stretch to donkeys!" said Mary.

Joseph lifted Jamie up onto it and handed him the baby, and so they made faster progress.

As Jamie looked due south towards Hebron, becoming visible at the top of the next hill, he saw another reason for courage to rise.

The star! The comet, low in the southern sky, just before the night sky faded with the dawn. There it was, exactly as Theo had seen it only a day before – tail directly upwards, head pointing down to Hebron. Going ahead of them, leading south to Egypt.

"Look!" he said in wonder. "It's Yeshi's star."

And so they made it to the outskirts of the town where no one yet was stirring, except two men, armed with swords, hidden by some trees, watching out for them – Zechariah and Rabbi Reuben.

And so they were escorted safely inside before the sun rose, to Elizabeth's hugs, and food, and hot water to wash their wounds, and comfortable beds.

"We didn't know what had happened," said Elizabeth, when they had told their story and grieved more fully for the Bethlehem babies than the harsh journey had allowed. "We just knew we had to pray, and that you needed us."

"We will keep praying," Zechariah assured them; "for you, and for those who have suffered such great loss. The Lord will bring comfort."

"Sleep now," said Elizabeth. "You're safe here."

Joseph and Mary went gratefully to their room with little Yeshi, but Jamie looked to the door, remembering the shouts of the guards in Bethlehem and that dangerous, puffed-up man on the couch with his darting eyes. *Were* they safe? With all his spies and thugs, couldn't his reach easily stretch to here?

"He would have to find you, and then he'd have to get past us," said Reuben, seeing Jamie's fear and setting a chair in the middle of the room, sitting with sword in hand. "He won't be able to do either."

Zechariah sat with his sword next to Reuben, equally determined; he looked as strong as a man half his age.

"The prayers of people God sees as blameless are powerful and effective," he said confidently.

Prayers, and an old man with a sword? Was that it?

"But... there's only two of you," said Jamie.

"Three," said Elizabeth putting John safely in a cot, then bringing her chair next to Zechariah and taking a long dagger from her belt.

"'A cord of three strands is not easily broken,'" said Zechariah, quoting from the Holy Writings. He saw Jamie's look of doubt. "What, you think Elizabeth and I are too old? How old were Moses, Aaron and Hur when they prayed-in a mighty victory for Joshua's army?"

"Ancient," agreed Elizabeth. "We're youngsters."

"Jamie, it's not just about what you can see," Reuben told him. "Those who are with us are far more than those with Herod. Heaven's armies are a mighty host."

"I've seen them," gulped Jamie, trying to remember and believe.

"Well then!" said Reuben. "The prophet Elisha knew that, when he was outnumbered by his enemies. All around us are the same invisible horses and chariots of fire that protected him. Go on, now. Off to bed."

And so they slept soundly until it was nearly dusk, with the prayers of their three guardians, and who knows how many more, wrapping round them like a blanket.

Chapter Twenty-five

THERE AND BACK AGAIN

The onward journey was so much better, now that they had the donkey. Their three friends loaded it up with water bottles, bedding and food so that they could camp out rather than trust to homes and villages, since they had decided to travel by night for a day or two more. It was a tearful farewell, but in a very good way, as they crept out of the house under cover of darkness feeling strong and encouraged.

Jamie couldn't help but feel excited as they travelled far beyond where any of them had gone before. The adrenalin rush as they passed Beersheba made him dizzy. He'd heard 'from Dan to Beersheba' so many times in Rabbi Asher's classes, meaning the whole land, since those were the towns at the opposite ends – so to know as they reached that southernmost point that they really were leaving Herod's territory made him want to break out in his customary travel dances again.

Joseph and Mary were a little more cautious, of course. This was still the Roman Empire, and plenty of people moved around it. They didn't want to stand out too much in case word got back, but they felt safe enough now to journey by day and use the roads the Romans so thoughtfully provided wherever they went. And yes, they let Jamie sing and dance sometimes, when there wasn't anyone else around.

"What about people we know?" Jamie asked as they moved steadily on. "Clop and everyone. And Dinah. Won't they be worried about us?"

"I told Eli we'd be staying in Bethlehem for a while when I wrote to say Y'shua was born," said Joseph. "I didn't say how long. He'll have told our friends in Nazareth. And with the rains starting soon, they'll think we don't want to travel. They won't expect to see us for many months now."

"And Dinah will think we've gone home to Galilee," said Mary. "Don't worry, we'll get a message to her when we want her to start baking for you again."

Jamie looked with interest at the wilderness between Judea and Egypt. This was where his ancestors had travelled back and forth, many centuries before:

Joseph, the dreamer with the multicoloured coat, sold into slavery by his brothers – jealous, what with him having snazzy clothes, and dreams that meant he was going to be a big-shot.

Then Joseph's brothers and his dad Jacob, needing help when famine hit, turning to big-shot prime minister of Egypt Joseph, not knowing who he was.

Finally the journey back, after four hundred years, during which they'd turned from a family of honoured guests into a large nation of slaves. God rescued them with mighty miracles, but it took them *forty years* to travel this desert Jamie was crossing now – not because they didn't have the benefit of Roman roads, but because they wouldn't trust God and wandered round for ages.

Jamie's family not having such problems, the desert didn't take them long – and then... they were in Egypt!

Reader, there were monkeys.

Pet monkeys; wild monkeys; monkeys on leads; performing monkeys. Even religious monkeys, if that's the right term. The Egyptians worshipped many gods, some of whom had human bodies with animal heads, and some of whom they believed could take on the shape of animals, including monkeys. So they liked to have a good supply of monkeys around, just in case. Baby Jesus squealed with delight to see Jamie engulfed in monkeys – running up his arms, picking his pockets, clambering all over him and perching on his head.

The Egyptians also had pet cats – lots of them, often with large, pointed ears; pet dogs; pet leopards, panthers and cheetahs, being walked by their rich owners as casual as you please. On one occasion, a pet crocodile on a lead. They even saw hippos bathing in the River Nile. No elephants or giraffes, but Jamie saw drawings of them which gave plenty of fuel for his imagination. He was in his element.

There were Jewish communities in many places, especially large cities such as Alexandria. Heliopolis even had a Jewish temple, run by priests who were real descendants of Aaron. It would have been easy to find somewhere comfortable and start a little carpentry business, but Mary felt strongly that they shouldn't settle anywhere, or mix too much with people from their own land. It was a wise precaution, so that they never got to be known by those around them; word would be less likely to get back to a neighbour's relatives at home.

This meant that they travelled around, living on the money the Magi had given them instead of working, and for Jamie it was like an extended holiday – although he wasn't happy to be surrounded so often by people he had little in common with. It's a wonder his nose didn't become permanently crinkled from turning it up at so many unfamiliar flavours of food. The donkey coped much better, becoming quite cosmopolitan in outlook – no longer batting an eyelid when expected to share a stable with camels.

There were so many things they had never experienced before.

They saw the *sea!* Jamie had never imagined there could be so much water – or that it could taste so salty, as he paddled and learnt to swim.

They saw the lush, green delta of the Nile, where the river split into a triangle of smaller streams, and they went upriver, further into Africa, where the land was scorched pale and dry, and the winter sun was hot.

They saw the nomadic, tented settlements of the

Bedouins, and bustling towns and cities so different in architecture from what they were used to.

They *even* saw the Pyramids and the Sphinx.

Jamie showed all this to baby Jesus, hoping he would enjoy the variety. Jesus gazed wide-eyed at everything, taking it in.

"Look, Yeshi," said Jamie one day, taking him down to the bulrushes by the river, making sure there were no suspicious-looking logs that could be crocodiles. "This is where they floated baby Moses in a little boat! A horrible king wanted to kill him too, and the other baby boys. But God hid him, just like he's hiding you."

The baby bounced in Jamie's arms and tried to grab a bulrush to chew on. He seemed to want to chew on everything these days, so Jamie carved him a teething ring, smoothing and polishing the wood like glass.

There comes a point, even on the best holidays, when you start to miss home. That is even stronger if, like Jamie, you allow sly feelings to take root in your heart that your country and your ways (and people like you?) are somehow superior. It felt as if they had been there a very long time when, just after Passover in Heliopolis, Joseph sat down to breakfast with a look that meant business, and they realised he'd had another dream.

"Herod has died," he said. "We can go back."

Mary and Jamie gasped, then Jamie had a thought.

"I don't know the angel's name," said Joseph firmly.

They skirted the edge of the Mediterranean Sea, right the way around the bottom corner, as they journeyed back to Judea, with Jamie dancing through his repertoire as little Yeshi chuckled, clapping him on. Jamie felt a great sense of the rightness and weighty meaning of going back. This made him just like Moses and his ancestors – going back to his own land; a much better land; the land where he would be prince.

At the border they stopped at a checkpoint staffed by a Roman soldier.

"Avete!" he greeted them in Latin, though with a local accent.

"Ave. Peace be with you," said Joseph.

"Pledged your allegiance to Caesar?"

"Yes, indeed," said Joseph, showing the little pottery disc from the census.

"All good," said the soldier, winking at Jamie. "Been away long? It's all change here. Herod's copped it."

"So we heard," said Joseph, as neutrally as he could.

"Good riddance," said the soldier.

Before, Jamie would have plunged in with an agreement, but the events they'd come through had taught him to guard his tongue. This man seemed friendly, but it could be a way to draw them in and trick them into saying something he could arrest them for.

"Mind you, his son's worse," the soldier went on. "Herod Archelaus. Makes his dad look stable. He's in charge of Judea and Samaria now."

"Not the whole land?" asked Joseph.

"Nah. They've split it in three, among his sons. Might've been four, but he finished off another of 'em just before he died. Can you believe it?"

"So, who's in charge of Galilee?"

"Herod Antipas," said the soldier, shrugging. "Dunno about him. But they're all Herods, ain't they?"

The family were quiet as they walked to the next town where they could find an inn, wondering what to do. Was the soldier right that Archelaus was worse? They'd been thinking of living in Bethlehem for a few months, so that they would be handy for the feasts; they'd had enough of travel for now! But was it wise to go back to where the scrolls said Messiah would be from?

"Let's pray for wisdom," said Joseph as they went to bed. "The Lord gives it generously to everyone, if they ask. We'll ask him to tell us where we should go."

"And, *this* time, will you find out the angel's name?" begged Jamie.

"No!" said Joseph.

So Joseph had another dream, putting him way ahead of the other Bible dreamer called Joseph, son of Jacob. In it he had a visit from an angel, who may or may not have been Gabriel, telling him not to settle in Judea but to go home to Nazareth. And that is what they did, hugging the Mediterranean coast all the way up the Via Maris, or Way of the Sea, until they reached Galilee.

They agreed on the journey that, while they would make trips to Jerusalem for the feasts, they'd never go to Bethlehem or Hebron, however much they longed to visit their friends. The city was safer. They could stay at Miriam's and see John's family there, but only go to the Temple when it was crowded so that there was less chance of bumping into people who'd remember them.

They also decided not to tell of the things that had happened: the angels on the night Jesus was born; the prophecies in the Temple; the Magi's visit – or, at least, not for many years. Not until Jesus had achieved what he'd come to do. Some knew who he was and some had clearly guessed, but it would be best not to keep talking about it. Rumours that the Messiah was here and had survived needed to die down until the time was right, if they were to avoid more attacks from the Herods.

"We'll treasure it up in our hearts," whispered Mary, seeing Jamie's disappointment – but treasure in your heart seemed a poor substitute for everyone knowing how important you were and how right you had been!

What a weird feeling it was, to be back in their home after all that had happened. To see it with new eyes, and settle back into life as it had been before, when they knew that really *nothing* was as it had been before.

Amazingly, there was the crib and all the baby things

179

laid out, which they had totally forgotten about.

"Welcome home, Yeshi," shouted Jamie. "You've got your own bed at last!"

Little Jesus said "Gaaargh!" and waved his arms and legs, throwing his teething ring on the floor.

"His bed, and *some* of his clothes," laughed Joseph, shaking the dust and cobwebs off them. "But look at the size of these ones. They're far too tiny for him now!"

"Oh, I'm sure we'll find a use for them before too long," smiled Mary in a Very Significant Way.

Joseph looked at her with amazement and delight, as if she'd just given him some fantastic news – though Jamie couldn't fathom what on earth it could be.

He guessed within another month or two of course, and as the years passed and Jesus grew big and strong, the crib and baby clothes were repeatedly put to good service, with the teething ring gathering gnaw marks from a succession of different bony gums.

Jesus and Jamie's brothers were called Joses, Simon and Jude. Their sisters were called Tally, Lilly, Lucy, Gracie, Robyn, Ffion and Sooz (you're right, I'm making names up again. The Bible doesn't tell us what their sisters were called, or even how many there were – only that they had some).

Jamie started out reasonably strong in his role as big brother, using his baby-care skills for bathing, burping and changing. To begin with, he diligently taught each child the words and routines to his songs as soon as they were old enough to totter after him. He was bound to get fed up with it, though. Having the Messiah throw up on your shoulder or squall loudly in the night is one thing, but it loses its charm with ordinary siblings.

I'd say – given all they had to go through to get to this point, and despite his *many* faults – Jamie did pretty well. And that is the end of this story.

Chapter Twenty-six

YOU HAD ONE JOB

Except for one thing.

It happened when Jesus was twelve and they went to Jerusalem for Passover as usual. Jamie wanted to be James now and got annoyed when anyone called him Jamie, so I shall certainly continue. He gritted his teeth as they tramped the road south, with most of his little siblings giving it large with "'I rejoiced!' (I danced and jigged about. I was very happy)". He had stopped teaching them his routines years ago, but it was too late; those he had already trained passed them on to the next batch with as much enthusiasm as he'd had when he was their age. They had a whole chorus line going that would do any musical theatre show proud.

Joseph noticed Jamie's glowering face and smiled serenely. "Revenge is sweet."

Jesus also grinned, sharing the joke with Joseph, which irritated Jamie even more. Jesus didn't always join in the line-up, but the boisterous, repetitive play of the younger ones never seemed to bother him.

If you were hoping the big-headed tendencies you'd doubtless spotted in Jamie might have softened over the years, I can only say that all that time of knowing he was the Messiah's brother didn't help. Neither did being nineteen. Not that the age of nineteen has a bad effect on everybody. Far from it; most of us get through it pretty happily. But it made Jamie feel responsible and mature, which fed into his self-important inclinations. He was a skilled carpenter, and thinking of getting engaged, which gave him a strong sense that soon he'd have his own home and business and would be in charge. As if that was ever what growing up or getting married was about!

Miriam was betrothed now – though not to Jamie, to his relief – and Cleopas and Tolomai had weathered the business of ending their teens and getting married with no ill effects. Tolomai lived in Cana now, a few miles from Nazareth, because his wife's parents had given them some land. Clop had married a young woman called Mary, and I must say, I'm disappointed in him. I'm sure, if he'd tried, he could have found a nice girl to fall in love with who had a different name. It's been tricky enough telling you *this* story; I've already cheated with Miriam. She was really called Mary too, so I've been calling her by the Hebrew version of her name to avoid constantly having to tell you which Mary I mean. But there will come a time – twenty years or so from this point, and in another book – when we will be *awash* with Marys, and I do think Clop might have had more consideration before he needlessly added another one.

Jamie's general moodiness as he trudged the long road with his family was added to by a frustration that they weren't *doing* anything yet to prepare for their mission. The whole dodgy-rulers-and-fake-high-priest situation was no better; Herod Archelaus had become so bad that the emperor Augustus eventually removed him and put Judea directly under Roman rule, but it felt as if nothing had really changed. There was a new high priest, called Annas – who was in the pocket of the Romans rather than Herod's, like that made any kind of difference at all. One non-descendent of the real high priests was much the same as another, as far as the ordinary worshippers at the Temple were concerned. And the first thing the new Roman governor did was another census! This time with sky-high taxes people couldn't afford.

There had been a ton of anger and unrest in the last two years, with rebellions breaking out. Jamie had begun to realise that it wasn't just Theo and his tutors who had done the math; some of Jamie's own people seemed to have spotted the clues hidden in the scroll of Daniel after all. Not everyone was aware of the prophecy, of course, but there were enough who had worked out that the time of this anointed ruler was getting near, along with what sounded like a golden age – an end to sin, and all the rest. They were looking around restlessly to see which of the rebel leaders it might be.

Jamie felt they should be training themselves up in fighting techniques so they'd be ready to harness the people's mood as soon as Jesus was old enough. But Joseph and Mary said it was up to Jesus; he would know the right time and way. They were much too laidback with him. He'd be thirteen this year, with the legal responsibility of an adult in Jewish culture. It was time he started stepping into his role, yet Jamie suspected they hadn't even told him who he was!

They arrived at Miriam's house in good time and unloaded the faithful donkey, whom they all thought of as one of the family. They were much earlier than they needed to be to choose a Passover lamb and observe the festival, because they also planned to work on the house. Many years before, Joseph had built a guest room at the back for Zechariah and Elizabeth, but now the small upper room his own family used was getting tatty, and it didn't make sense to keep patching it up. It was only big enough to house Mary and the smallest of their children (Flopsibelle, Lavinia, Barry and Keith); everyone else had to camp out on the roof. Joseph had discussed it with Matthan and Dinah on their last visit and offered to make the whole of the flat roof into one huge room. It would benefit his own family when they stayed, but also meant their hosts could hire it out to large groups in between, so everyone was happy.

The project went well, with Joseph, Jamie and Jesus taking the main responsibility for the skilled jobs, and everyone else helping as they could. Jamie had to admit that Jesus always set himself fully to whatever he did – even if Jamie would have preferred that to be sword fighting, spear throwing and riding lessons.

Jamie found something unnerving about his brother Jesus, despite the dutiful way he worked and his great popularity. Something in his eyes; an uncomfortable feeling of not knowing what he was thinking – especially of not knowing what he thought about Jamie. He was irritatingly wise (unlike Jamie at that age), yet without seeming at all boastful (unlike Jamie at that age), and, although he never disobeyed, he didn't show the respect Jamie felt an older brother deserved from one so much younger. If Jamie advised him on something – anything – he always felt Jesus politely acknowledged it, then decided for himself.

This unsettled feeling was far worse whenever he met their young cousin John. Jamie got a chance to experience that sensation many times during the feast, as of course Elizabeth and Zechariah were there too, and the families spent much time together.

John didn't speak often; he watched. The. Whole. Time. Whenever Jesus was around, he showed the same fascination he had as a baby, listening to all he said – but he watched other people too. His eyes were like gimlets, the tools a carpenter uses for drilling a hole through stubborn wood. Jamie knew it was probably because John had received the Holy Spirit – which made him feel even less comfortable – and part of John's mission to prepare people for the coming Messiah – which was an outrage! Jamie was the Chosen One's brother; he didn't need his heart preparing by some kid, thank you very much.

What with dodging Jesus and John, second-guessing what they thought of him, and his natural resistance to

Temple offerings as payment for his sins, Jamie tried to keep his head down and his focus on carpentry.

He was relieved when the religious observances and building work alike were completed and, early on the morning after the feast finished, they stopped off at the Temple to make their goodbye offering then left.

As they passed through the Damascus Gate and along the road, the weight started to lift. It would be good to get home where he felt less under pressure, less as if everything he did was being analysed and found lacking by a couple of adolescent boys. He decided that from now on he'd concentrate on setting up his own home; that made him feel more certain and in control. Blocking out the in-flight entertainment provided by his younger siblings, he talked himself up in his mind to a state of greater confidence.

That feeling was dented next morning with a reality check, when they had to step aside to let a cohort of grim, fully-armed soldiers pass. This particular rebellion was nearly over, crushed by Rome, but Jamie took comfort that Jesus was called to succeed where all the others had failed. Their mission was all that mattered, and Jamie couldn't pretend he would be able to bury himself in an ordinary life, not after all he'd seen. He was stirred anew with an impatience to get going, and looked around to see if Jesus was showing those same emotions at the sight of the oppressive Roman soldiers. If so, Jamie could encourage that and help him to realise it was his destiny.

Jesus. Where... actually... was he? Jamie looked up and down the straggling line, not to see if the Romans were provoking a buried call to action – just trying to spot him. Which part of the group had he been in as they walked? Or as they camped last night? Or... as they set off yesterday? Jamie's skin went cold and his stomach turned. Had Jesus *ever* been with them at all?

Oh, no. No no no no no. Trying not to panic, he pushed his way back against the flow of dancing children to where Joseph walked, in conversation with a couple of their neighbours.

"Dad... Dad!" Jamie interrupted. "Where's Jesus?"

"Jesus?" asked Joseph. "Why, he's right... "

He looked around vaguely, and saw that Jesus wasn't right anywhere. Jamie ran quickly to the front of their group, where Mary was trying to stop Jude and Talitha annihilating each other with a snake they'd found.

"Where's Jesus?" asked Jamie breathlessly.

"With your father," said Mary, without even turning round.

Jamie looked up ahead to where Cleopas and Tolomai were walking with their wives and Tolomai's parents; he sprinted to catch them up. Joseph, seeing his lack of success, ran back hopefully to Mary's mother, chatting with two of her daughters, and beyond them to Eli, walking with some of his other grandchildren.

"Have you seen Jesus?" yelled Jamie, his urgency stopping Clop and co in their tracks.

They turned to look at him, the young women not bothered, the rest unable to believe it.

"You've lost *Jesus??!*" said Clop, aghast – and on their faces the subtext screamed *the MESSIAH??!*

"I know, I know," said Jamie, pelting further ahead to check with Mary's other brothers and their broods, then back to join his own family. As he got to Mary, who was also starting to realise she couldn't remember when she had last seen her miraculous, firstborn son, Jamie heard Eli at the far end of the line shouting "You've lost *Jesus??!*" and Joseph replying "I *know!*"

They assembled at double speed, doing a quick head count this time, and set off to Jerusalem with strictly no dancing as, far behind, Clop yelled "*Seriously??!*"

It was no use, when they got back the next day. They'd hoped he would be at their lodgings, since that was surely the obvious and sensible place to wait if you got separated from your family, but Miriam, Dinah and Matthan hadn't seen him since the morning they left.

Miriam stared gravely at Jamie, not sure he understood the seriousness of the situation.

"You've lost – "

"Yes!! We've lost him. I know," snapped Jamie.

It felt very personal, as if they were all somehow blaming *him*. Jamie wanted to shout dramatically "Am I my brother's keeper?" but he knew the answer was "Well... yes." He had always felt he'd been given a sacred trust. And anyway, it wasn't a good quote. It was from the story of Cain and Abel, so it would make Jesus like faultless, unjustly treated Abel, and Jamie his guilty, blood-stained brother Cain. *Not* a comparison Jamie wanted to bring down on himself.

They left the children with Miriam and searched everywhere they could think of – the well; the fruit sellers; the butchers; the cheesemakers; even the place they'd bought the wood; all the streets of the old city – he was nowhere to be seen. Long after dark they collapsed into bed, exhausted, at a loss what to do.

Next morning, they could hardly touch any food as they discussed their options.

John was seated in a corner waiting for his parents to come through for breakfast, reading a Hebrew scroll – neither worried nor surprised, which was even more infuriating than everyone else's reproaches.

"Have you looked in the last place you saw him?" he asked casually as Jamie passed him. "Just sayin'."

Jamie stopped, trying to think. Where *had* they last

seen him? He'd definitely been with them as they went to the Temple... and in the Court of the Gentiles, after their offering, when they said goodbye to John and his parents... and after that?...

"Dad, what about the Temple?" said Jamie urgently, going over. "That's the last place we saw him."

"Great idea! Well done," said Joseph, and he and Mary eagerly grabbed their cloaks.

Jamie was about to say that it had been John's great idea, but then thought that it probably didn't matter too much who got the credit so he didn't need to bother. He became aware of John's piercing eyes looking right into him and casting a light on things he'd rather keep hidden. Jamie wasn't going to stay and justify himself to a thirteen-year-old, so he hurried after his father.

The Court of the Gentiles had a different feel from usual. The trading was more subdued, and all the street performers seemed to have gone on vacation at the same time. Most people were gathered loosely under one of the colonnades where rabbis sometimes assembled to debate the law or teach their disciples.

Jamie and his parents scanned the people, trying to remember what Jesus had been wearing – when had he disappeared, three days ago? – when they heard a light, clear voice they recognised instantly.

"When it says 'Love your neighbour like you love yourself' that's a very royal law. If you break it, even just by being snooty to someone, you've kind of broken the lot. You'll be judged one day, so make sure you show people mercy in the meantime. Top tip: mercy always wins over judgement! And it's not just mercy. *Everything* good and perfect comes from the Father of the heavenly lights, and he doesn't change, like shifting shadows. His perfect law gives freedom, but there's no point just staring at it – you have to actually do what it says! Otherwise, it's as much use as gawping at

188

yourself in a mirror then forgetting what you look like."

They pushed through the approving crowd as if they were in a trance, unable to believe that here he was, speaking so calmly, after all their desperate efforts.

"Well said, young rabbi!" laughed another familiar voice – an old friend they hadn't seen since the night they fled from Herod.

"What about you, Rabbi Reuben?" asked Jesus. "How do you see God's law?"

"I suppose – " pondered Reuben, silver-haired now, and then broke off as he saw Mary, Joseph and Jamie emerge at the front of the crowd. "Of course!..." he breathed in wonder, as it all suddenly fitted into place.

Jesus was sitting cross-legged with a group of rabbis in a circle, as if one of them. Had this been going on the *whole time?* So much for keeping a low profile.

"Son!" said Mary, hardly able to find the words. "What are you doing? – what were you thinking? Didn't you know your father and I would be frantic with worry?"

Jesus looked at her, seeing that she was upset, processing her words, and yet not affected by them in the way Jamie felt he certainly ought to have been. His eyes, so open and honest, moved over to Joseph, taking on board that she had referred to him as his father – turning that idea over in his mind to test what he thought of it. Whether it was true.

"Why were you worried?" asked Jesus. He wasn't being cheeky; he genuinely seemed not to understand their problem. "Didn't you know I'd be in my Father's house? Where else would I be?"

Jamie was furious at this insult to Joseph, after all he had done for the ungrateful boy, but Joseph stepped in.

"No harm done, eh? Come on, Y'shua. Time to go."

Jesus got up straight away, thanking the rabbis for

189

the interesting discussion. He gave Joseph a big hug and a contented smile, and they left with Mary. Reuben looked over at Jamie, filled with joy, shaking his head, moved almost beyond expression.

"Well, now. Wasn't that something!" he murmured.

Jamie nodded to him with gratitude for the past, wishing he could see things the way Reuben did. But all Jamie could see was that somehow, somewhere, everything was going off track. He was glad Reuben had enjoyed meeting Jesus; that was lovely, of course – but there were urgent things they should be doing. It was time to *start*, and no one else seemed to realise that.

He followed Joseph, Mary and Jesus back to Miriam's, moodily silent, trying to work out the best plan of action. It didn't help, when they got there, that everyone crowded round making a fuss of Jesus instead of sitting him down and telling him straight how dangerous and foolish his behaviour had been.

John didn't crowd round, of course; he looked up from reading his scroll to watch Jesus as usual, neither relieved nor surprised. It hit Jamie that John was part of the mission too. Getting him fired up might help.

"It's time to prepare, don't you think?" Jamie said to him quietly. "He's growing up. Maybe he should start to step out in what he's called to do."

"Maybe he just did," said John.

What a ridiculous thing to say! Jesus was supposed to be bringing the kingdom in, not sitting round chatting about God.

"I think we should get ready to go for it," Jamie persisted. "This uprising, rebellion vibe that's in the air. People starting to look for Messiah. The time is right."

John mulled over the idea.

"Priests and Levites start serving God when they turn thirty," he commented, as if that were somehow relevant to warrior kings.

Jamie huffed in frustration, not about to let it lie. If no one else was willing to take responsibility, it would have to be down to him.

"I've got to be more assertive," he murmured – to himself, more than to John. "Dad's way too relaxed. I need to take a firmer hand and show Jesus the kind of things he should be doing and the way he should go."

"Yeah. Good luck with that," said John.

Appendix: Prophecies, Dates and Leaky Tents

That really was the end of this story; you honestly don't have to read any further unless you want to find out more about the history behind it. A book's appendix has nothing to do with a squashy organ in the bottom right corner of the stomach – it's just an extra bit! I said I'd tell you how I think Daniel's prophecy works out to mean that 'the time of mashiach' would be thirty years after Jesus was born. It's a bit complicated (understatement!), so as a bonus I'll also tell you why I didn't put Christmas in December, where Jesus was born and whether the moon really turned pink.

First thing: It's tricky being sure of exact dates from so long ago. (You don't need to remember any of this, I'm just going to show why it's hard to pin things down) There are gaps in our information. Or sometimes it only comes from one historian back then, and how do we know if he was careful to report things accurately? How can we even be sure of the way they counted?

How we count is not as simple as it seems. If, at 2pm on a Monday, I said something would happen in 3 days... well, Monday, Tuesday, Wednesday – that's 3 days, right? I meant it would happen at some point on Wednesday. Or did I mean 3 full periods of 24 hours? That would be 2pm on Thursday. If you weren't sure:

a) you could ask me;

b) you could guess from what you know of my personality – how precise or laidback am I with words?

c) you could guess from the culture I live in – what do most people like me mean when they say that?

But if it was said a long time ago, then a) is impossible and b) and c) are very difficult. Even if I'd tried to make it clearer by saying "within 3 days," "in exactly 3 days" or "after 3 days" – if I'd lived 2,000 years ago and my language was now dead and only pieced together from fragments of inscriptions and coins, it would be hard for you to know for certain what those words meant in my time and place.

In ancient history, things are often dated as being a certain year of a king's reign, or so many years from a famous battle. But we have to look at whether they mean from the actual anniversary date of the battle / the king coming to the throne, like we do – or from the current year (even if the date was only a few days before the end of it) – or from the start of their next new year (even if the date was 11 months before that would happen). The king might have been in power for less than a month then it was suddenly his second year – or for 11 months before they even started counting! Some cultures reckoned their years from the autumn equinox, some from spring, some from January; some had several types of year (like us, with financial and school years as well as the January one). And how are they numbering them? A baby is zero years old for the whole of the first year of its life, then it stays one year old for the whole of its second year, and so on – so which way of expressing numbers does this culture mean? We could easily be out by a whole year, on that alone.

And don't get me started on rulers who reign together. Near the end of his life, for instance, Augustus officially made his stepson, Tiberius, co-ruler of the Roman Empire with him. So, if a Bible writer or a historian from that time says "In the 15th year of Tiberius Caesar" do they mean from when he was made co-ruler, or from around 2 years later when Augustus died and he became the only emperor?

And there were many different calendars, some based on the moon, some on the sun. Some added a leap day occasionally to keep in sync; some added a month, less often; some didn't bother, and let their dates drift further from the seasons and everyone else's dates. They hopped onto the calendar we all share now at different times, and they made different adjustments to do it.

Even days are measured differently; some cultures reckon a new day starts at sunset, some say midnight...

Everything is therefore based on studying what we *do* know, plus educated guesses and interpretation. This is how I came to my interpretation:

Daniel's Prophecy

According to Daniel 9, verses 24-26, Gabriel brought a message to Daniel in exile in Babylon, 'in the first year of King Darius', 522 BCE (Before Common Era; same as BC. The years go backwards, as it's a countdown to when Jesus was thought to have been born):

"A period of seventy sets of seven has been decreed for your people and your holy city (Jerusalem) to finish wrongdoing, to put an end to sin, to pay for guilt, to bring in everlasting righteousness, to confirm or 'seal up' prophecy, and to anoint the Most Holy Place. Now listen and understand! *Seven sets of seven plus sixty-two sets of seven will pass **from the time the command is given to rebuild Jerusalem** until a ruler – an anointed one – comes.* Jerusalem will be rebuilt with streets and strong defences, in dangerous times. *After this period of sixty-two sets of seven, the anointed one will be cut off and have nothing,* and a ruler will come whose armies will destroy the city and the Temple."
(That's mostly the New Living Translation. I've added italics and shouty bold to show what we're discussing)

When was the command given to rebuild Jerusalem? There are four that could be meant, and these are the dates most historians agree on:

538 BCE – Cyrus II (Cyrus the Great) had permitted some of the Jews to return and rebuild the Temple, and gave them money and the objects which had been taken from it. It started well but was stopped by opposition.

521 BCE – Darius I checked and saw Cyrus's decree,

so he confirmed that they had permission to rebuild the Temple. This time they finished it, and the Temple was re-dedicated in 516 BCE, 70 years after Jerusalem was destroyed. (A different prophet, Jeremiah, had said their captivity would last 70 years!)

458 BCE (some historians reckon 457-455) – Artaxerxes I gave Ezra, a Jewish leader, money and instructions to take charge of Jerusalem, appoint judges and reinstate God's law. Ezra and his group started rebuilding the city, but again, there was opposition.

445 BCE (or 444-442) – the same king, Artaxerxes I, noticed that his Jewish servant Nehemiah was sad because Jerusalem was still in ruins. He gave more money, and permission for Nehemiah to rebuild it. There was still opposition – they had to build the walls taking it in turns, half of them working, the other half on guard with swords – but eventually they succeeded.

In brief, 4 orders: a command to rebuild the Temple; a confirmation of that command; a command to restore the city; a confirmation of that command. As Gabriel's message was about the city, not the Temple, I think it's reasonable to pick the third one, the command to Ezra.

Gabriel said that 7x7 and 62x7 (483) after that, an anointed one would come and cool stuff like everlasting righteousness and an end to sin would be achieved. If we add 483 years to 458 BCE, we end up in 26 CE / 26 AD (there is no Year Zero. I know; don't blame me). Hmmm. Did anything interesting happen in 26 CE?

We need to look at what year Jesus was born. Although BC means 'Before Christ' and AD is from the Latin for 'the year of our Lord', the turning point was calculated 500 years after the events by a monk called Exiguus, who didn't have as much historical information available as we do now. (He's the guy you can blame for not making a Year Zero! Honestly, Exiguus)

The ancient historians who mention Jesus and John the Baptist (Josephus, Tacitus and Pliny) tell us who was ruling at that time and who was ruling the followers of Jesus a little while afterwards. What they say ties in with more detail in the Bible: who was ruling where; what year of their reign it was; who was high priest, and so on – both when Jesus and John were born, and when they were around thirty. If you combine all those things, it works out that Jesus must have been born in 5 or very early 4 BCE. I'm going with 5 BCE.

The answer is, therefore: *drumroll*
Jesus turned thirty in 26 CE.
(Or if scholars who think the command was a year or 3 later are right, the prophecy still lands in his ministry)

In the story, I had Theo and John hint that this would be important, but we'll cover it properly in book three of this series. If you *reeeeeeeally* don't want to wait that long, you could skip ahead by reading Luke 3:21-23!

(This message from Gabriel is one of many parts of the book of Daniel that predict the future, and I ought to mention that some people don't think they're real, because they are so detailed and accurate it doesn't seem possible. They think the book was written only 160 years or so before Jesus was born, not around 550 years. 168/7 BCE was another time the Temple and city were damaged (the events of Hanukkah), so the theory is that it's only *pretending* to prophesy things that had actually already happened, to encourage people, and especially their brave leader, as they fought an oppressive ruler.
Some parts *are* about that oppressive ruler, whether it was written at the time or hundreds of years before. But regarding the message Theo talks about: It occurs to me that if the writer was making up that it had been written

long ago, wouldn't they have picked a different number of years, instead of 483, so that it would add up to the time they wanted – 168/7 BCE or fairly soon after? It doesn't seem to, by anyone's dating system. Another thing I wonder about is the idea of 'mashiach nagid' being cut off and having nothing, and then the Temple and city being destroyed. If the writer was trying to inspire and encourage the brave leader and all the people fighting the oppressor, they weren't doing a very good job. Surely they'd have made it a happy ending? The only way it makes sense to me is if that bit isn't about the 160s BCE but a different time, a little while after 26 CE, and the cost of paying for guilt and the rest of that amazing list was higher than anyone guessed.

Looking at a different way of checking the date of the book of Daniel: By around the 160s BCE, and possibly earlier, a number of other books were quoting Daniel; it had been translated (and some words were already so unfamiliar they were translated wrong), plus there were many copies of it. That wouldn't be a big deal now, but in the days before printing presses and trains, cars, planes, never mind the internet, it took time for a book to spread so far and become well known.

And even if Daniel *was* written in the 160s BCE, some of it was still predicting the future anyway. There are spookily accurate descriptions of the Romans, who hadn't happened yet. Plus, of course, our favourite bit about 'the time of mashiach' works out at 26 CE, quite a way into the future – then 'afterwards' he will be cut off – and then the city and Temple will be destroyed by another ruler, which did happen, in 70 CE.

Oh, and Jesus called him 'the prophet Daniel', so he certainly didn't think the book was pretend prophecy!

Those are the reasons I think the predictions are real)

What time of year was Jesus born, and where?

Phew. If you've read this far, you must be as much of a history geek as me! In which case, you might be wondering why I put the birth of Jesus at the Feast of Tabernacles in September, rather than in December, when most of us celebrate Christmas?

The Bible doesn't actually say when Jesus was born, and God didn't tell us to celebrate his birthday; it's up to us whether we want to or not. A lot of people *did* want to, so they picked a date – since, if you believe that Jesus being born was a good thing, you could really celebrate it any day! But it probably wasn't December; it says there were shepherds out in the fields overnight, and December is during the rainy season in Bethlehem.

I could simply have picked a random date to use in this story, but there are a few clues in the Bible. The festivals in the Old Testament often seem, to followers of Jesus, to have an echo in the New. I've thought for years that the Feast of Tabernacles, celebrating God's presence coming down to inhabit the Tent of Meeting, sounded *very* much like what I believe happened at the birth of Jesus. The Bible talks of tents as a symbol for the body. They're movable; they give protection; you live in them (and the living thing is far more amazing than the tent itself). They wear out in time, becoming faded, baggy, wrinkled, creaky, torn; bits go missing; they start to leak... all right, that's quite enough of that comparison. The point is, a tent is a good metaphor for a human body, so how hugely appropriate Tabernacles would be for the birth of Immanuel: God with us, sharing our human condition and living in a tent.

I found out that other people think Jesus was born at Sukkot too. But to put it in a book, even a fictional one, I wanted to check it out further. John the Baptist was born six months before Jesus; when would that be? Passover. Well, that works nicely; the prophet who would come in the spirit and power of Elijah was kind of expected then anyway – people often set an extra place for him at their Passover meal! When would Jesus have been conceived? Hanukkah, or the Feast of Dedication (another event God didn't *tell* us to celebrate but many people want to, including Jesus, when he lived on earth). That's a celebration of God's miraculous provision of light, so again seems very appropriate.

But the big clue is Zechariah being part of the group of Abijah. From the Mishnah (very old Jewish writings, interpreting God's law) and one of those historians of the time, Josephus, we get a picture of how the priestly rotas worked. King David had put them into twenty-four groups, and apparently in Zechariah's time they served for one week, twice a year, working for eight days so that they overlapped – two groups on duty every Sabbath. At the great feasts, all priests and Levites were on duty. Abijah was the eighth group, and because Josephus tells us which group was on duty when the Temple was destroyed in 70 CE, we can work out when the rota started each year. It looks as if Zechariah's group was on duty right after the Festival of Weeks, which means – whether it happened during the festival as I've put it, so our friends are there to see it, or in the days after, during his ordinary service – the timing would be perfect for Gabriel to appear to Zechariah in the Temple, him to go home after his duty week, then John the Baptist to arrive just over nine months later.

So that decided me on choosing Tabernacles – which is what made the year 5 BCE not 4, because Herod almost certainly died around Passover in 4 BCE, and he was still alive when Jesus was born.

Was Jesus born in Migdal Eder, the Watchtower of the Flock? We don't know. All the Bible says is that he was born in Bethlehem, and Mary laid him in a manger because there wasn't a guest room available. Heaps of places had mangers; they were very free and easy with allowing animals in the house in those days, and I'm not talking dogs or hamsters. Some families let their sheep, goats and other animals sleep inside, so they might have a manger in their living room.

Within a hundred and fifty years of the birth, one writer was saying it happened in a cave near Bethlehem; a hundred years later, locals were pointing out the very cave to tourists. But even if that's true, the cave could have been the basement of an inn. Or a tower?

Migdal Eder, the watchtower where Jacob's family camped, *was* very near Bethlehem (though we don't know exactly where) and Micah *does* say lordship and the kingdom will be restored there, only seven verses before the famous "But you, Bethlehem Ephrathah" bit. And I had to pick *some*where!

Finally, were there really total eclipses of the moon the nights both John and Jesus were born? Aaah, that was the cherry on top of all my research, by accident, when I was looking into something else! The death of Herod, in fact: Coins and inscriptions point to 4 BCE, and Josephus said it was between a time of fasting / a lunar eclipse and Passover, so I was checking out lunar eclipses in that part of the world for the years around that time. There was a partial one at Purim, celebrating Queen Esther's story which includes fasting, in mid-March, 4 BCE, so that was probably the Herod one. But I suddenly spotted that there was a total lunar eclipse at Tabernacles in 5 BCE, on the exact day I had already written about Jesus being born! And *then* I noticed that there was also one at Passover in 5 BCE.

It's not mentioned in the Bible, we don't know when Jesus and John were born anyway, and I've seen no one else point out those eclipses in connection with their births. But I think lunar eclipses are beautiful and I'd already chosen those dates, so I put it in!

Printed in Great Britain
by Amazon

33919065R00125